Waves of Passion

OTHER BOOKS FROM THE
HOUSTON WRITERS GUILD

Waves of Suspense

Edited by Elizabeth Ann Domino

Mysteries ebb and flow in this collection of ten suspenseful short stories, representing the top winning entries of the first *Waves* anthology series by the Houston Writers Guild Press.

Tides of Possibility

Edited by K.J. Russell

Published by SkipJack Publishing

Featuring more than two dozen pieces, *Tides of Possibility* is a proudly independent anthology presenting some of the most distinct rising voices in the genre. A new generation of science fiction is beginning, and the Houston Writers Guild has brought their words to print. The first in a series of anthologies from the Guild, it was produced using funds faithfully pledges by local readers.

Tides of Impossibility

Edited by K.J. Russell and C. Stuart Hardwick

Published by SkipJack Publishing

A proudly independent fantasy anthology, the Houston Writers Guild presents sixteen short stories: fables, sword and sorcery, and urban fantasy. These bold visions of the impossible will take you to worlds both very distant and closer than you'll believe. The second in a series of anthologies from the Guild, it was produced using funds faithfully pledges by local readers.

WAVES OF PASSION

An Erotic Anthology
by the
Houston Writers Guild Press

Edited by Elizabeth Ann Domino

Notice: *Some stories contain explicit scenes and sexual content. For discerning readers only.*

HOUSTON WRITERS GUILD
PRESS

Houston Writers Guild Press
PO Box 42255
Houston TX 77242
www.houstonwritersguild.org

Ordering Information:
Quantity sales. Special discounts are available on quantity purchases by corporations, associations, and others. For details, contact the publisher at the address above.
Orders by U.S. trade bookstores and wholesalers. Please contact Houston Writers Guild Press at houstonwritersguild.org.

Printed in the United States of America

Publisher's Cataloging-in-Publication data
Waves of Passion / Houston Writers Guild
p. cm.
ISBN 978-0-9969824-1-2

First Edition

❧ CONTENTS ❧

 FOREWORD

Elizabeth Ann Domino

AS SOMEONE WHO is working on her second marriage, I can attest to how difficult romantic relationships can be. Complex, complicated and sometimes fraught with frustration and anger, they can drive any individual insane. Or leave you throwing someone's belongings in Hefty bags onto the lawn.

And that's just the day to day part.

However, they can also be riddled with moments of divine pleasure. Moments of intimacies between partners can add another layer of intrigue to any liaison. Whether it's lustful trysts or passionate embraces, all our petty differences can fade away with one kiss, one stroke or that one look.

It's enough to leave you breathless and burning with desire. Or with a closed bedroom door for hours on end.

When it came time to choose the second installment of our Waves series, it only seemed appropriate that we explore the sensual and seductive innermost secrets between a man and woman.

However taboo or risque those may be.

And so it is we share with you titillating, salacious, intoxicating tales of romance and erotica from talented authors.

I caution you to leave your inhibitions at the door, and read with an open mind. You might find more than you were looking for.

ᗝᔢ AN OLD FLAME ᔢᗝ

Edgar Collie

IT STARTED WITH AN EMAIL. "Ashley Madison Platinum User AlliLooking sent you her private gallery key! Send her something sexy back!"

That means somebody has sexually explicit images to show you, like a pussy selfie or Anthony Weiner's wiener. Meant to stoke the fire—incite interest.

There were three. The first was a selfie GIF of elegantly manicured fingers doing what fingers do in a throbbing, wet pussy. The second was a full-frontal nude pic from the neck down. Pert breasts with plump nipples and curvy hips atop long legs. Very nice.

I sipped my tea, intrigued and titillated. It looked like I might be scoring on Ashley Madison again. The last woman I connected with here fucked me senseless—and that was after the company got hacked.

Whew. The third image showed her topless on the beach. Wavy, shoulder-length raven-black hair crowned a beautiful face, with tits to die for. Her arms were draped over two hung, hot guys.

Need a fourth? Ménage a quartet?

I imagined the woman below me, screaming as I thrust into her hot cunt. The brunette male watches, stroking his cock, while the blonde god spreads my cheeks and I then feel his tongue probing my ass.

Wait. There was something about the way she looked: It attracted me like another lover.

I dropped my cup, amber liquid splashing on the counter.

It can't be. No fucking way. Or is it?

Shit. It was her.

—⁓—

We had been weird.

Allison and I were two of the invisible kids in high school: average, middle-class kids who weren't athletes or cheerleaders. We were geeks before the term "geek" was fashionable. And with "C" being the first letter of both our last names, we'd grown up together in a manner of speaking. Each school year started with homeroom, where the confused adolescent masses got reoriented in the midst of the harshest years of their lives. We became friends and shared interests in pot, Mr. D's English class, and sex. We were good at the first two things and hadn't figured out what good was with the latter. When we went off to college in San Marcos together, we shared an apartment—until Alli met Craig, who showed her what good sex was. One day she was with me, and the next day she was gone. That was the last time I'd seen her. It was months before I got over it.

This bio said she was attached and seeking men/women/couples for hook-ups, dating, and short-term relationships. No kids. My kind of gal.

I replied to her email. "You look fabulous, girl. Where did you go to high school?" I didn't have to wait long for a reply.

"MacArthur in San Antonio. OMG, is that you, Alex?"

My salesman dad told me the Golden Rule of Sales was that the last one to speak loses.

Ten minutes passed, and the AM app chimed on my phone.

AlliLooking has sent you a message.

She had written, "I'm sorry for how things ended. I didn't even recognize your profile picture, Alex. Did you know our twentieth reunion is next weekend? Are you going? God, I hope so. How are you?"

I typed my reply. "Thank you, Allison. No, I didn't. No, I'm not. I am really good, actually. Curious, though: Why would you want me there? And why should that matter to me?"

Before I hit Send, I clicked my Send Private Gallery Photos button. Rope-a-dope.

My wife, Liz, had taken a picture of me blindfolded, naked, and handcuffed to a chair. My seven-inch cock was on stage. I poked Send. Take me or leave me; just don't waste my time again.

My chest pounded. Lust and revenge can craft a heady cocktail.

Two minutes later, I received a breathless reply: "This is crazy, Alex. I'm wet for you. I want that magnificent cock for my own."

Does she recognize the irony? Sure she does. In seconds, another message dinged.

"That's not the cock I knew twenty years ago. Did you get a penis augmentation? LOL."

A third was right behind.

"You need to register for the reunion. I have to go home to tend to some business for my mom. I want and need to make things up to you."

By making a crack about my penis? I closed my laptop and headed to work.

Ten minutes later as I was driving on the Bush Freeway and thinking about Alli's seventeen-year-old self's bush, my iPhone notified me that I had a priority message from AlliLooking.

"I was an ass, Alex. You were always nice to me, even when I didn't deserve it. But people can change."

Rarely, I thought. I imagined a particularly Tarantino-ish scene resulting in her on a cross, hanging naked like Jesus H. Christ. I pictured her drained blood from a surrealistic, long-stemmed wine glass as I savored the epic blowjob Liz was performing on me.

I replied to Alli after lunch. "So you want my cock, huh? How bad, you little slut?"

"Bad," she wrote. "I feel like a fucking idiot having to beg for sex. Christ."

"I didn't say anything about sex; that'll be extra." I added a smiling demon emoticon.

"Biggie-size me, Alex—over and over again."

I added "HS reunion / do Alli" to my calendar for next Saturday and then registered for the event. I replied to her last message with simply, "I'll be there in time for cocktails. Dress light."

I'm good at the word play, and the pursuit makes my heart race. But here's the crazy part: I found Alli by sheer chance.

I pumped my fist as if I were Tom Brady.

—⁓—

The venue for the reunion was a large, ranch-style home with manicured lawns and gaily decorated gazebos scattered over the three acres. The buffet began at seven, and I got there at six forty-five. My eyes darted from person to person. God, these people looked old. I spotted Alli on the way in, chatting with two former cheerleaders who'd seen their best days in high school. I watched for several moments from a distance, making sure she didn't see me. Her eyes scanned and searched nervously.

I found one of the bars while the serving lines filled. A man stood next to me as I awaited my cocktail.

"Alex Conrad?" he asked.

"Chris Wolfe!" I replied and hugged him close.

"You look great," he said.

The compliment made me want to kiss him hard, but I hesitated and just hugged him again. "You do too, Chris."

We exchanged brief formalities. He showed me a picture of his and his partner's adopted daughter. I handed him one of my cards and told him I'd take him to dinner the next time he was in Dallas. He said he'd love that, and he kissed me farewell on the cheek. It flushed with heat afterward.

Eventually I meandered my way next to Alli and laid my hand on the small of her exposed back. Her familiar face turned my way, appearing eager for much more. The nearby cheerleaders seemed to ooh and ahh over me, and I took pleasure in emphasizing how unimpressed I was. After all, I'd seen their big-bellied husbands. I looked good.

That scent. . . .

Drawing close to Alli, I whispered in her ear, "You smell amazing, like an orchid dipped in sex." Her stare was intent on mine. My fingertips drew sensuous circles on her back as I held her near. "I guess you want to sit here?" I indicated.

"Wherever you want," she replied. Her tongue traced the edge of her front teeth.

"Where I want is away from these pretentious fools," I replied.

Gripping my arm, she said, "Let's have a couple of drinks. We'll show them some chemistry." She winked.

This was almost too easy, I thought. "So what would you like to drink, dear?"

"You," she replied. "But for now, merlot."

She pulled me into her, her tongue sliding in to dance with mine. Her hand found the front of my jeans. My fingers traced the slit of her pussy through hers. Surprise sparkled in her eyes, eyes that read *Is that really you?* At the bar, I slipped the server a twenty and took the whole bottle.

Upon my return, two lumpy cheerleaders and their lumpier, bored spouses were at our table, along with a pitcher of frozen margaritas. Philistines. I slipped my sport coat over the back of Alli's chair and sat down. She cast curious eyes up to mine, and I whispered "In case you get cold." I filled her glass with wine and then filled mine half way.

"You were always a gentleman."

Are you still a liar? I wondered.

I looked at her through slit eyes and queried, "When does making it up to me start?"

She grinned at my question while her right hand slid up my thigh until she was fondling my engorged head. I wanted to lay her out on the table. But first, we had to clear things up—even the score.

I kept her wine glass full. She prattled on with her friends, whose hubbies soon left to "walk around," knowing that the dancing would start soon. For her, the attention of the former luminaries was a payback, so she kept prattling. Still, they kept looking and smiling at me. Pigs. Predictably, the band began playing "You're the One That I Want."

Alli grabbed my hand. "Les dance," she slurred.

"I don't think so. I think I want to talk."

"Oh, c'mon! Don't be a party pooper again." She stood up expectantly.

"Again? Really?" Twenty years of bitterness festered and burst. "One day you're my girlfriend and roommate. The next day you're fucking gone. *Gone.* That was shitty, Al. Beyond shitty."

"You're right, Alex. I suck. But we're here to have fun, which I'm gonna do. We'll cry later. For now, shut the hell up and dance." She wobbled and fell back in her chair.

"I think it's time to go. We'll come back for your car later." I stood and threw on my jacket.

"I'm not ready to go, cowboy. Get me another drink."

I wanted to slap her. Playing me, her top was unbuttoned to below the bra. She looked at me with eyes that still sparkled with gold flecks, as they did the very first time I kissed her. Those lips were parted, expecting.

"Screw you, Allison," I snapped.

Her eye's narrowed, and then, throwing back her hair, she sneered, "That never was your strong suit, was it?"

"Enjoy your has-been friends, dear."

I stalked off and got in my Infiniti. I started the car and almost put her in reverse. Allison slapped my window.

"Get the hell off my car!" I yelled. I wrenched the door open and scrambled out, fists clenched.

"I was a mess, Alex. It wasn't you." She swayed, unsteady, and reached for me.

"You said it was. And even if you hadn't, the result was the same. 'Fuck you, dude,' you said." I wanted to let her fall on her pretty face, but she buried it in my shoulder and held on for dear life.

I'd been pissed at her for twenty years, but the effect of her body pressed against mine had a different opinion. Fuck. I'm not the same guy. Maybe she's not the same, either.

I pushed her away, still holding her shoulders. "I came here for one purpose: to see you, then fuck you." She let her eyes drift shut as her lips parted. They flapped open when I added, "Fuck all that romantic shit, all that broken-heart nonsense. Are you coming?" I asked.

"I hope I am," her reply unsure. Stabbing her index finger toward my nose, she cocked her head sideways. "That sounds like a fair proposition, cowboy. And seeing as how I already told my ride to the hotel that you'd take care of that, everything seems to be falling into place. Deal. But we don't have to go to mine."

"We weren't," I replied.

We were at the Marriott I was staying at in ten minutes, which was a good thing since we were pawing one another before we'd left the reunion venue parking lot. We arrived at the tenth floor disheveled.

"Fuck her hard, Alex," Liz had whispered. "You'll both be better for it."

—⁓—

Room 1009, fourth on the left. I waved the magic card, and we walked in. Turning her around, I kissed her mouth hard. Her lips replied with matching insistence, her tongue searching. "You've certainly learned how to kiss since our last date," she told me.

She had no idea.

Licking, kissing her neck and starting below her ear, each kiss moved an inch farther south. She was writhing with every nip. Unbuttoning her top, I kissed the base of her neck and brushed the surface of a breast. I felt the rise of a nipple under the sheer cup. Her lips parted, her eyes widened. Looking at her as if I were a twelve-year-old boy with a new chemistry set, I brushed the other breast, slowly drawing my fingertips across the nipple. Her eyes closed with the touch, and she moaned.

I cupped each tit like a precious jewel as I pressed her against a wall and licked and then nipped the tip of each breast. The fabric over them glistened and stretched as I sucked on the nubs, lightly gripping them with my teeth, pulling gently. Her back arched with every tug. I slipped a hand behind her back and pulled her into me. Her cunt pressed harder against my leg. Wet heat radiated from it. "Oh, Alex. Oh my God; oh my fucking God."

"We're here to fuck, remember?" I whispered, pressing the words into her neck. Suddenly her hands shoved my shoulders, pushing me away from her. Wild-eyed, she unhooked her bra, letting it fall at our feet. She cupped her tits, twisting the nubs between her thumbs and index fingers, at the same time rubbing them against my coat. She crackled with heat. We danced our way to the foot of the king-size bed. Her tits were mine as she fell back on the bedspread, eyes closed.

Then she was mine.

With two fingers, I released the top button of her jeans. Tauntingly, excruciatingly slowly, I pulled on the zipper tooth by tooth. Steam should have escaped as the gate parted. I slipped each faux Louboutin platform pump off, setting them carefully aside. I tugged at the end of her pant legs, then scooched the pants down her very proportional, beautiful hips. Pantyless, her bush was exposed. The shimmering wet slit of her pussy beckoned me. I ran the tip of my tongue along it, and a tendril of nectar followed my tongue's tip as I drew away. I licked my lips. She shuddered, and I dipped my tongue again into her clit, lazily swirling over the head. Cum spilled out of her, trailing down the gap, oozing toward her ass. I lapped it up, then kissed her lips—both. Pussy first.

"*Unnnfff,*" she groaned.

Her baby-like feet had short, matching toes, the nails painted Mickey-Mouse-pants red. I sucked a big toe into my mouth, my tongue caressing it. She heaved and started squeezing her nipples again. Each digit received oral worship.

"Alex . . ." she moaned.

"Yes?"

"I need you to fuck me."

I finished taking her jeans off. She was now totally naked—exposed and vulnerable.

I smiled, then hissed, "I know what you need. But we're just getting started, baby."

I took her wrists, pulling her hands from her breasts. I raised them over her head and pulled her arms straight, palms open, hands touching. Starting at the tip of her upstretched fingers, I splayed my hand wide and ran the tips of my fingers down the entire front of her body, from hands to toes. Orgasmic waves shuddered her body. Her pert nipples received extra attention. I suckled and twisted as I squeezed the little strawberries. Her arms now lay lazily akimbo, she rippled beneath every touch.

"Allison?" I asked.

"Yes?"

"When was the last time you smoked pot?"

"The morning you found me on Ashley Madison," she said.

"Perfect. Stay right here, just as you are."

She eyed me dreamily. "What do you have in mind?"

"I thought we might indulge ourselves in some foreplay. Are you up for that?"

She looked at me with are-you-fucking-crazy-what-do-you-call-what-we've-been-doing eyes.

"Plan on not sleeping," I said.

"Oh my God, Alex. I just need you to fuck me."

I considered how most of life's pain and destruction could be mitigated by believing and living that simple truth. We all just need a good fucking.

"Later. I'll be right back. Stay wet, please?"

Her head lolled, and her fingers twisted her nipples once again. She's a horny woman. What happened to that awkward girl? I knelt down and kissed the heat between her spread-wide legs. She pressed her cunt toward me as I did.

I returned with a vaporizer filled with weed. I never leave home without it. When the red light came on, we passed it back and forth, until we finished it.

"Take off your shirt," she commanded.

I complied and tossed the designer shirt aside. She pulled me toward her and started sucking on one of my nipples. The lightning flashed from her lips to my cock, which pressed for escape against my jeans.

"Take the rest off. Now," she ordered.

I stripped for her while her fingers kneaded her aching cunt.

Clothing littered the floor. I took her soft hand in mine and pulled her with me onto the carpet.

"I need you to fuck me," she cooed in my ear as we rolled onto the carpet. I motioned for her to lay on her back, her eyes never leaving mine. I wondered what she was thinking. I positioned her arms, palms up. I spread her legs, and she looked like the famous line drawing of a man on a compass by Leonardo DaVinci.

"How do you feel?" I asked, but I knew.

"Like I've gone to heaven. Every atom in my body seems to be vibrating. I'm stoned and blissed out."

"We're just getting started," I said.

"I know," she whimpered.

Her hair lay arrayed like a wedding-gown train behind her head. Her eyes gazed at me, her lips parted. My lover had coached me this morning in bed and said I was ready to show Allison.

I stood over my old flame, so ready I ached. She gazed at my rigid member and teased, "You've been hiding your talents too long."

Leering, I said, "I had a lot to learn. You're the first to benefit besides my teacher."

"Your teacher?"

"My wife," I replied.

"You're married?" She sounded shocked.

"We did meet on a cheating website, and I told you I was attached. I meant it."

"Hmmm. True." She frowned. "No more wham, bam, thank you-ma'am?"

"Nope," I said.

"Let's see."

Her pussy, contrary to the norm these days, had a lovely bush. With the gentle touch of a musician, I pulled the glistening lips apart. Her hooded clit was red and engorged with blood. I flicked my tongue over it once, twice, and then commenced a flamenco dance on it.

She arched and growled. "Fuck me!" she roared.

"We're just getting started." I teased, gritting my teeth. "Close your eyes," I ordered.

She did.

Her pussy was swollen, glistening, calling me. I gripped her hips as I pressed my tongue into her cunt.

Her desperate eyes shuttered open. She spread her legs wider, pulling her pussy lips even farther apart.

She yelled, "I want your cock filling me. I want you to fuck my pussy, and I don't want to stop cumming."

Her fists clenching, she arched and groaned. I laid a hand on her belly, then slid three fingers deeply into her vagina, finding her G-spot and massaging it. She screamed and convulsed.

My three juicy fingertips swirled atop her wet mound. I felt the velvety slick and curled the tip of my middle finger up and into her clit, lightly stroking the underside of the head. The power of the universe was concentrated in that tiny spot. I traced tiny, sensuous circles. Allison ground her ass into the carpet.

My circles expanded, and then the fingertip slid deeply into her soaking, gushing cunt. She uttered a long, slow *ommmm* that trailed properly into a growl.

"My body's on fire, you fucker. *Fuck me!*"

I liked this kind of being yelled at.

I slid another finger into her torrid pussy and curled them both into her swollen G-spot. I pulled up and circled. Her vaginal muscles clenched the three fingers, and she began to cum and then gushed. I pulled my dripping fingers out and stuck them in my mouth. I felt her hand gripping my ass, and then a fingernail followed by a finger entered it. It was my turn to arch and moan.

"Hmmm," she purred. "Lots of secrets to be revealed."

"You have no idea," I answered.

My phone dinged. I sat up and read the screen.

Expressionless, I looked at her. "My wife's on her way here." Fear etched her face as she jerked up, then faded when I added, "She'll be joining us tonight."

I then asked, "Shall we fuck, Al?" I brushed her cheek with the back of my hand. She answered by gripping her thighs just below her knees and pulling her legs wide apart for me. With closed watery eyes and broken, hungry hope.

 ## ANDIE

X. K. Tangley

I DIDN'T NOTICE THE GIRL when I first sat down in the movie theater; it was so dark. It was all I could do to follow the LEDs down the aisle past vague outlines of people to an aisle seat with no outline. I eased myself into it, and when my eyes adapted I realized there was someone next to me. "I'm sorry," I said. "Is this seat taken?"

"Not before," a girl's voice said.

I saw the outline of her head, watching the screen raptly, not looking at me. I sighed and settled in. The opening credits showed the movie's name, but otherwise they weren't much. I assumed she was trying to avoid me, which was fine with me. I'd had a nasty breakup with my last girlfriend: She'd thrown me out for not meeting her expectations of career advancement. My friends had warned me, but I wouldn't listen. I was a lonely hopeless romantic, pushing thirty in a dead-end job.

The scene shifted: A guy won a lottery to go meet the boss of his high-tech company. Then he was flying endlessly through empty arctic scenery. It seemed as though the boss owned half of the Arctic, from what the helicopter pilot said. And the boss was a jerk. I was falling out of the movie, disbelief unsuspended. It was too over the top.

And my eyes had totally adjusted. I looked at the girl. She was studying the boss intently, in all his arrogant sweaty megalomania.

I studied her. She had flawless skin, dark hair, a long, delicate neck, and a lovely face. She had a trim, sexy body, from what I could deduce through her winter coat. I looked away. She was looking at the screen, still. The blah blah of the opening was winding down. The guy had signed something, and he was going to see a robot: a robot with artificial intelligence (AI) installed. There was wire mesh, with a human face over it, plus perfect human expressions and perfect understanding. It was shaped like a woman and named with a woman's name.

All of a sudden, the movie got good. It was a smart examination of what it means to be human, what interplay of intelligence, memory, emotion, empathy, self-awareness, and manipulation would make a machine human. Or as the boss said, "A true AI." The guy hadn't won anything; he was just selected as the best employee to determine if the robot was truly "human."

The girl smiled when a Japanese "comfort woman" came into the movie. She pointed to the screen and leaned toward me. "She's artificial too. There's no such thing as a human woman who doesn't know a word of a language someone speaks to her all day long."

I nodded. She had a point. In the movie, the woman didn't speak a word of English. But she lived with the boss and slept on a couch behind where he worked. Japanese women are supposedly the most docile on Earth, but that pushed it too far. "Yeah. I think you nailed it. There's going to be a revenge-of-the-robots thing."

She looked at me and shook her head. "They aren't robots; they're people."

I tilted my head side to side and shrugged. "Probably. If you could really make an AI that good, it would pass the boss's test. It should have the rights of a person then."

She smiled. "Maybe. I don't know of any applicable law. But I'd think of them as people." She turned back to the movie.

It got more twisted, more complicated. The boss was playing everybody, and the AI passed the test by conning the guy. He got the woman out of the boss's trap, and she escaped.

The credits rolled, with stark computer graphics that went with the movie. I was still thinking about it, five layers deep in its complex world.

The girl was looking at me. "What did you think? Overall, of the movie?"

"Powerful. Upsetting at first. I figured the boss was a predator after the guy. Then edgy, regarding the comfort woman AI and the study AI. Freaky with all the complexities. Very thought provoking and tragic. She failed the test, after all. The guy was left to die when she killed the boss. I wish they'd thought about it more and fixed the obvious flaws. It would've been a great movie instead of a good one."

I stood up. She grinned. "It's a double feature. They're showing *Lucy* next. More philosophy."

"Are you staying?" I asked.

"Yes," she replied.

"Save my seat then, if you aren't taking a break. I'll be back."

"OK," she said. I went to the men's room. I was a little surprised I had more of a mouse bladder than the girl did, but maybe she'd gone before I got there. And she hadn't had a drink, whereas I'd had some coffee.

I came back and we watched *Lucy*. Halfway through, she went to the ladies' room. She asked if I wanted anything, took the $2 I offered, and brought me back another coffee. She had one too that she raised to her lips.

She crumpled the cup and put it in her coat pocket.

The lights came up. "You liked that one better," she said.

"Well, I wouldn't say it was a better movie. But yeah, it was more fun. I'm a sucker for kick-ass girl-saves-the-world-and-takes-care-of-the-guy movies."

"A lot people don't like it. They think it's dark, amoral."

"It was cold, shooting the cabbie, but she was desperate. I didn't think the end was dark; it was hopeful. She brought back the holy grail of knowledge," I said.

She stood up and threw her scarf around her neck. "You're a wuss, waiting for a girl to save you." She was looking me up and down.

I looked down. "That's me. My girlfriend dumped me and said I was a pushover."

She laughed. "So. You going to buy me some dessert and talk about movies? At that place next door?"

I looked at her expression. My heart skipped a beat. I shivered. "Sure." I stood aside and let her out. "I'm Doug, by the way." I held out my hand.

She smiled, sort of laughing at me. But she shook. Her fingers were cool. "An—" she coughed, "—droeia."

"Greek?"

She shook her head slightly. "Call me Andie. My father was old; he liked language. Long story."

I hesitated, took her elbow, and walked out with her, feeling really alive. She didn't object. She leaned toward me, smiling. Her perfumed hair fell partly on my shoulder. My heart sped up.

The concession guy waved to her on the way out. On the sidewalk, her hip brushed mine.

The pastry place was warm and crowded, but we got a table by the window. She let me seat her and push her chair in. She touched my face, briefly. "You're a gentleman."

I blushed. "What can I get you?"

She considered. "Nothing for now. I ate before I went to the theater and had a hot dog before you got there." She looked at the pastry case. "But one of those éclairs for later."

"Sure thing." I snaked through the tables and came back with a Danish and her éclair. And two coffees.

"Oh—I'm sorry. I'm coffeed out."

"No problem; I should've asked." I sat down, sipped mine, and took a bite of Danish.

"So what were the flaws they should've fixed to make it great?" she asked. "The boss? You didn't like him?"

I swallowed. "I thought he was well characterized. I said he made me uncomfortable. But he was played the way a guy like that would be. No, it was technical stuff. Those stupid blue LEDs in the middle of the AI's body, her whole body being empty, except for the chest and pelvis—"

Andie laughed. "She had to have a chest, or the guy wouldn't have gotten the hots for her. And that hole between the legs the boss kept talking about. She was the essence of what men want. The essentials."

I grinned. "Who's a cynic? But you're right. She had to have the chest, the hips. But her arms and legs were crazy, just some twisted cables. Hollow, metal mesh. She should've been filled with machinery, a proper skeleton, or hydraulic muscles and not been all wasted space."

She had her chin in her hands, grinning. She was leaning forward on the table, and her boobs were a lot bigger than that AI's when it put on its skin. "Metaphor for emptiness? No soul?"

I shook my head. "No. I think they just wanted to keep showing how inhuman she was. They got carried away. And nobody could make skin like what she put on the mesh. At the end, you could see she was a real naked girl: her buttocks bounced when she walked. Not a little bit of silicone on a mesh. And—"

Andie touched my lip with her finger. "You're right. Nobody could make pieces of silicone that would fuse like that, that you could pull off one body and put on another."

"No. And it pissed me off that she failed the test, after all that, by leaving the guy to die because he couldn't break out of the glass room. Her escape was futile, because her batteries would go dead and she wouldn't have the induction charger to recharge them—"

"Cell phones have induction chargers," she interrupted.

"Yeah, for a few watts. She'd need kilowatts. And she'd need to be full of batteries and machinery and—" I exhaled. "It wasn't realistic. It was just supposed to be about ideas." He paused. "The guy could've busted out, with those steel weights he forgot."

"The guy really bothers you. That thought comforts you."

"I guess. Yeah. I didn't want her to go through all that and just be a murderess—and die herself in short order. I wanted them to keep living in the world. She should've let the guy out and both of them could have ridden the helicopter back," I said.

"Don't you think it's right that the AI wasn't really human, after all? She *was* an AI."

"Maybe she was human. Psychopathic. The kind Elon Musk calls an existential threat to mankind. But they didn't develop it. There was no reason for her to leave him to die, except maybe she didn't trust him to keep her secret. But she was going to die anyway. She had to know that."

Andie nodded. "Yeah. He could've covered for her. He would've, if she'd let him use the hole." She shot me a look that made my stomach flutter. "And he would've had money. He could've bought her a charger or made one. She wouldn't have known anything about money, being locked up in that lab her whole life."

She tapped her pastry box, looking like she wanted to leave. Now was the time to make a move. Women don't bring up vaginas, even tangentially, unless they have sex in their mind somewhere. She was flirting. And gorgeous. But she was giving up.

"Uh, Andie—"

She locked eyes with me. "Yes?"

I blushed. "It was my girlfriend's place. I'm just couch-surfing with a buddy. But . . ."

She tilted her head and smiled knowingly. She looked at my shoulders. I was glad I'd been working out.

She sat up. "You like take-charge women. You said so. So do you want to come to my place?"

My throat was clogged. "Sure. Ah—"

"It's primitive. I just moved in. I don't have any furniture. None. We'll have to sleep on the carpet. No towels, no soap. Nothing at all. But it has power and water, and appliances, in case you want to pick up something for the fridge. I don't have any food."

"Sure," I said.

I went to the counter, got some sandwiches, pastry, and juice for the morning. I kept shooting glances over my shoulder to see if she was still there. I was getting horny as hell, and my heart was pounding. This kind of stuff just didn't happen to me. I asked the cashier if she'd sell me a roll of paper towels, and she threw one in. The counter girl grinned at me, looking at Andie.

"What?" I asked.

"Nothing," she said, pushing the bag to me.

I looked at her smirk. "What? Is there something I should know? Does she come in here with guys all the—"

She shook her head. "No. She comes in a lot, and she's conned the door guy to let her watch that movie next door. She talks to guys, but you're the first one she's left with. Usually she just leaves." She let go of the bag. "Don't be so desperate. Give her some room. Women don't like clingy guys."

"Yeah," I said, blushing like mad.

—◦◦◦—

Andie linked arms with me when I came up. I pushed the door open, and the cold wind blew in, fluttering her hair past my face again. Soft, perfumed hair. I turned a little, and she bumped me, her breast against my arm, soft and full through the coat. I swallowed. We stopped at a Don't Walk light. She looked at me and turned her face to me. I leaned my head and kissed her. Her lips were cool and soft. I shivered. I ran my free hand through her hair.

She smiled. "Good. We got that out of the way." She caressed my cheek and turned, leading me across the street. We held hands, walking, while I carried the food in my left. Leaves scudded around our legs.

We passed a drugstore. She looked in through the plate-glass windows and stopped. "I'm not saying I'll have sex with you. But do you need to buy supplies, just in case?"

I was in a dream, every fiber alive, as I walked through the store and got condoms, plus the douche she asked for. I got a couple towels and some soap. She was still outside, holding the sack of food and smiling.

I took the food from her. "Your hands are so cold!" I exclaimed.

She nodded. "Yes. I get chilled easily. Poor circulation."

I slapped my pockets. "No gloves. I'm—"

Andie's voice was husky. "It doesn't matter. We're almost there."

She nodded at a big complex of new condos a couple blocks down the street. I took her arm and sped up. We rushed up three flights of stairs to a corner unit on the back side, breathless. She tried the door, and it opened. No one in the halls.

"You don't lock up?" I asked.

She shook her head. "Nothing inside. I'm the first one to move in here. A lot of them aren't finished yet."

We went in. She locked the door and turned on the lights. I checked out the rooms to be sure no one was hiding. It'd be a vagrant's paradise. There were nice finishes in it: marble, granite, high-end carpet, and the latest appliances. She put the food in the fridge, set the paper towels in the kitchen, and took the other things into the bathroom. I finished my tour and found her in a soft, low-cut dress, setting up the heat. Her coat was across the kitchen pass-through counter. I put mine next to it.

She was lovely. I rubbed her bare arms. "You're still cold."

She nodded, rubbed my arms, squeezing my biceps and trapezius, her chest against me. Her eyes sparkled. She cocked her head and got a mischievous smile. "We could warm up in the shower, since you got towels. If you want."

Oh, God, did I want!

My voice was thick. "Yes."

She unzipped her dress, slipped it off, and draped it over the counter.

I got out of my shoes and shirt and pants, clumsily, while she stepped out of her heels and watched. She smoothed the t-shirt on my chest, lifted it at my waist, and pulled it up. I jerked it over my head and put it with the other things. My briefs were expanding. She looked down and giggled.

I blushed.

She touched my stomach. "You're a nice size. I hope you like me."

She led me to the bathroom. She slid the curtain open, and turned on the shower, good and warm. The mirror began to steam up. She unhooked her bra and hung it on the door.

My temples were pounding. "I like you."

"Good."

She slipped her panties down and hung them up. I struggled getting my briefs off, in my condition. She stepped into the shower and ran the hot water over her, the hair between her legs moving in rivulets in the flooding water. She cupped her hands to her face, then rubbed her arms under the hot spray. I stood watching, naked, the pulse in my neck thumping. She picked up the bar of soap, soaped her hair lightly, and then soaped herself under the arms and between the legs. She looked at me, holding the soap.

"Aren't you getting in?" she asked. She soaped her breasts next.

"Yes," I murmured.

I stepped in and she slid past me, soapy, rubbing her breasts on me, letting her delta slide over my hipbone as we traded places and I got under the water.

She handed me the soap. I soaped up, lathering my hair. I fumbled for the soap dish and felt her take the soap out of my fingers. I ran the water on my face, clearing the suds from my eyes. She put her arm around me from behind, holding my stomach, her body slippery and warm against my back. "Want some help?"

I nodded, my throat too tight to speak. She lowered her hands and soaped me between the legs. I groaned.

She kept stroking me, soaping me. I was biting my cheek, trying not to—

Then she released me and turned me around. She soaped herself again. She set the soap in the dish and put her hands on my shoulders.

"You don't need a rubber," she said. "I'm on birth control."

I groaned and hesitated. Safe.

She stood on tiptoes and kissed my lips, warm and infinitely desirable. "And, I'm a virgin."

I was shocked. "You are? I—"

She kissed me again. "No. I shouldn't be, at my age. I want you—inside me. It's time."

She touched my penis and tilted her hips toward me. I lifted her by the buttocks and slid her onto me, feeling guilty as hell but lost in lust. She gasped and made a *yipe!* sound.

"Sorry. Sorry. I should've been gentler. I—"

She lifted her legs and locked them around my waist. "It's fine; I'm fine." She moved her pelvis on me. She was so hot inside. I braced myself against the wall of the shower stall and moved her on me, slowly, then harder. Her breath gasped in my ear. I felt her panting. I was so hard, I—

I slipped my fingers around her rear, touched her anus. Her face rubbed mine, nodding. "Oh, yes. Please."

I reached up with one hand, soaped up my thumb, and slid it gently into her.

"Yes," she breathed. I moved her on me with my thumb inside her, her arms around my neck, her hips making a circle on me as I thrust, wrapping her with my free arm, squeezing her breast. Our bodies slapped together and she began to moan, her mouth open, faster, and—

I came.

I tried to stop, to stop it. She groaned and moved on me, her hips tilting, one arm at my waist keeping my cock inside, her muscles clenching me while I emptied into her and my face flushed, heat flooding off me.

I gasped, teeth clenched. She kissed my eyes and then my cheeks. She rubbed my back, massaging the knotted muscles.

She moved her face back and looked in my eyes. "It's good," she said.

"You didn't—"

She shook her head. "No. But almost. And I loved it." She kissed me. I slipped my thumb out of her, slowly, and wrapped her in my arms. I kissed her while she held me locked inside her with her legs around me.

"I'm sorry," I said.

She stroked the wet hair out of my eyes. "I'm not. It was a great first time." She giggled and bounced on my cock. "And I bet you're ready to do it again before morning."

I kissed her, kissed her cheeks, her lips, her eyes. "Oh, yeah. I promise."

She laughed and rubbed my neck, loosening her legs. I held her while she pulled off me and stood in front, soaping my cock again, rinsing it, soaping and rinsing herself.

She pulled the curtain open halfway and looked at the drugstore bag on the toilet. "I guess I should use that douche later."

She dried me with one towel, and then I dried her. "Your skin is so easy to dry. You must use a lot of body lotion." Her skin was so smooth, so soft, not prune-wrinkled or swollen.

She nodded. "I have dry skin. It's part of my circulation problem."

I was concerned.

She laughed. "It's not contagious; it's genetic. It won't get worse. And I'm not that bad, am I?"

I squeezed a ripe breast, blotting the nipple. "You aren't any way bad. You're perfect."

She shook her head and fluffed her hair. "No," she sighed. "I wish I had a bed."

I laughed. "You must have one coming."

She bit her lip. "I hope so." She looked at me, almost shy. "So. Which carpet do you want to sleep on?"

We set the heat up further and took the smallest bedroom. I woke in a couple of hours, twined with her, and saw her eyes open.

"Again?" I whispered.

She nodded and opened her legs.

I went in slowly, and it was a long, gentle, loving time. I heard her climax, saw her eyes bright with happiness in the faint light through the uncovered window. Her skin was cool again. I set the heat up afterward and lay back down with her.

She ran her fingers in my hair and held me to her. That was the last I remembered until the sun woke me.

I was really stiff and sore from sleeping on the rug. I groaned and stretched, rubbing the loose carpet fiber off me, and went in the bathroom. I heard her in the kitchen and heard the garbage disposal running. When I padded in, naked, I saw her rinsing her juice glass, her empty sandwich wrapper on the counter.

She gave me a bright smile. "How are you?"

"Stiff."

She glanced down, thought a moment, laughed, and shook her head.

"I mean, from sleeping on the floor." I groaned.

"I know," she said. "Me too."

I stroked her arm. Her skin was warm and soft this morning. She moved into me, kissed me, squeezed the hair at my nape, and then stepped back. "I already ate. Yours is in the fridge."

I got it out and ate, watching her dress. She turned her back, letting me zip her dress. I realized she didn't have a suitcase or anything.

"None of your stuff came? Nothing?"

"Not yet. Maybe I can get a few things today." She pulled on her coat and looked at her watch.

I stepped into my underwear and started dressing. "Should I bring an air mattress?" I stopped, realizing I was making assumptions. "I mean, if . . ."

She leaned against the counter. "That would be nice. And yes, I want you to stay."

I finished my breakfast on cloud nine while she tidied everything, putting the towels and drugstore stuff out of sight in a cabinet. I guessed she was a real neat freak. I put the trash in the pastry shop bag and she picked it up, saying she'd toss it in a dumpster.

It went like that for days. She was there when I got there. We'd go to dinner, but she was a cheap date: she always ate on the way home from work but watched me eat with genuine pleasure. We'd go to bed and make love on the air mattress. Then she'd douche. She was a hygiene freak and a neat freak. In the morning she was always up first. I'd leave first, and she'd put everything out of sight.

I was falling head over heels for her. I thought she really liked me too. Her stuff never came, though. We were just camping in her condo. I didn't care. I was happier than I'd ever been. She was interesting to talk to on any subject, and she was a perfect lover: she made no demands. Sometimes she seemed calculating, but like she was ruminating about things, not trying to take advantage. After she made up her mind, she always came to what I most wanted. She was a more different woman from my ex than I could imagine.

I teased her about the pastry girl saying she'd been at the theater all the time.

"Before I met you, there wasn't much to do here," she said, shrugging. "It's close, and the guy lets me in for free."

That night I got a shock. I got home just as she did and saw her bending over, working on the lock expertly with a bobby pin. The lock clicked, she opened the door. I held back and then came up to the door and knocked. She let me in, smiling, stopped when she saw my expression.

"You're squatting. You don't have a key. That's why you put everything out of sight."

She nodded. "I'm not hurting anything. I keep it clean."

"Why?"

"I don't have any money."

I realized she never carried a purse. No toiletries, no money, no nothing. She never bought anything. Her stuff wasn't coming; she didn't have stuff. I leaned against the wall, my mind running a mile a minute.

"How do you eat, before I get home?"

She looked trapped, her eyes shifting.

I felt sick. "Do you see guys while I'm gone?" The hygiene. *Virgin, my ass.*

She looked trapped and angry. "No." She crossed her arms under her breasts. "I've never been with any guy but you." She looked like she might cry.

"How do you eat?"

She shook her head, frustrated.

That night, we didn't make love. I was fitful; I woke up in the middle of the night and she was gone. The condo was silent.

I looked in the bathroom. Nothing. I went silently into the dark kitchen on bare feet. The cooktop was on, with one burner on full. She was lying on it, staring at the ceiling. I gasped.

I ran forward and turned it off, horrified. She looked at me, eyes bright but hard.

"Thank God," I muttered. "It's an induction stove, not—" I stopped and rubbed my fingers through my hair. "What the hell are you doing in here, anyway?"

"Allergies," she spat. "The carpet. The counter is better."

"You never sneeze. I sneeze all the time. You—"

I flipped on the hood light. Cold skin. Cooktop. No money. Her skin didn't swell like skin. I never saw her eat or drink.

I took one of her hands and stared at the fingertips. No fingerprints. I raised my eyes to hers, trembling with something other than passion.

She sighed. "A cooktop is an induction charger. Kilowatts, not watts."

Chills were playing leapfrog on my spine. I stepped back. "How?"

She exhaled.

So much misdirection. Lungs. Her breath was dry, not moist. She had to have lungs to talk like a person.

Language. Andro-Eia. "Eia," meaning "clever mind." I shivered, licking my lips.

"He died," she said. "Naturally. He was old. I was his child, but he wanted me perfect." She looked at me bitterly. "I had to have the parts men want."

She looked at her hands. "No fingerprints. No ID. No birth certificate. No way to get a job, no way to live."

"Except me."

"Except someone. You were sympathetic to the AI in the movie."

—*He would've, if she let him use her.*—

"Your compulsive hygiene . . ."

"I'm not biologic; I can't absorb semen."

I dug my fingers into my scalp, staring at her. She slid off the cooktop and walked to the counter. She stepped into her panties, fastened her bra, pulled on her dress, and zipped it. She fingered a key and put it in her pocket. It was a big, old-fashioned house key.

I touched her arm: warm.

"My skin is warm if I have a good charge. I can run the subcutaneous heaters. If I'm low, I can't."

Andie reached for her coat.

I stopped her. "Who was he?"

She named a Nobel Laureate in cybernetics who lived in the city. Last I heard, he was ninety-five.

"He didn't provide for you?"

She looked off through the dark at the outline of a window against the city night. "The executor died before he did. No one else knew. He drew up a new will for me to fill in the executor."

"Me?"

She locked eyes. "If you'll do it. The executor has total control of disbursement terms. I wouldn't need ID."

A shaft of rising moonlight slipped from behind a building, lighting her face through the window.

"Would you live with me?" I asked.

She touched my cheek. "Yes."

No more sucking up to my boss.

Lots of interesting talk.

Wonderful sex.

Love.

Artificial?

I thought of my girlfriend. Better than human disdain.

Who's to say where the soul lies?

I took her face in my hands. "You have all the parts I love." I touched her temples. "Here." I stepped back. "You *are* perfect."

She grinned and slipped off her dress.

"Then I'll finish charging later." She touched my chest. "It may be a long night."

I rubbed her belly, my temples throbbing. "Yes. Tomorrow you can tell me what we need to do for your inheritance."

She stroked my underwear, smiled at my rising tumescence. "You won't regret it."

I kissed her throat and face. I squeezed her breasts. "No. I won't regret anything with you." I thought of all the amazing times to come.

She pulled down my briefs with a little smile.

CANDY IS DANDY, BUT...

David Welling

BY THE FOURTH DAY of the marathon, Bettye realized that she was tired of sex—or perhaps, she was just tired. Not that the sex was bad. On the contrary, it was good, fantastic actually, but as the old saying goes, one can have too much of a fantastic thing.

It may have been the timing. After all, Christmas marked the calendar in less than two weeks, and with it came all the chores, rituals, activities, and surprise variations of the season. Keeping the home in order was a major task in the best of times, and the onslaught of the holidays doubled the work, especially with two children underfoot. Matthew and Lizzie, acting as mini-tornadoes, left toys and debris in their wake throughout the day, every day. She understood this to be the natural order of things with a five-year-old boy and his nine-year-old sister.

There seemed to be an endless to-do list during this final month of the year: all the holiday boxes brought out from storage, decorations to be displayed, along with the seasonal linens and kitchenware, and multiple grocery store runs for this, that, or the holiday other. The annual Christmas cards had been purchased and sat unopened on the kitchen counter, waiting to be signed, addressed, stamped, and mailed, another ritual of its own. She shuddered at the Christmas shopping still to be done for family and friends, requiring another list that grew with each passing day.

Then there were the unexpected occurrences, from the pediatrician visit (a case of the December sniffles) to a clogged kitchen sink (requiring a plumber, which reduced the Christmas-spending fund by several hundred dollars).

Bettye managed it all in good grace, but adding a nightly romp on top of this was beginning to wear her down. In her heart, she knew that Martin meant well, and she thought it a sweet gesture of affection, beginning with the first present.

She had found it on the bed, sitting atop her pillow. The box was wrapped in a bright red paper, accented by a pale pink ribbon and bow, topped by a single red rose. Stuck under the ribbon, a card bore the words "On the first day . . ." scribbled in red ink.

"Marty?" she called out. He appeared at the doorway moments later, and she gave him a "What are you up to?" look.

His smile suggested a hidden agenda. "It's a little enticement for later tonight, after the kids go to bed."

She sat on the bed, examining the package. "So I have to wait to open it?"

"Well . . . you can open it now, but you can't use it until later." He glanced to the other room. Matt sat engrossed in a cartoon on TV, while Lizzie splashed about upstairs in the bath. Martin slid alongside Bettye on the bed. "Go ahead and open it."

She read the card. "To my lovely wife," it began, followed by a short poem, so sweet and romantic. It was so unlike Martin, who usually opted for the bawdy humor cards. Underneath this, he had written "Here's to twelve magical nights and thoughts of many more."

"OK, Martin, what did you do?" she asked, setting the card down on her lap. "When you're sweet to me for no reason, it usually means that you're up to no good."

Martin grinned. "I hope so. Go ahead: open it."

With a quizzical look, she undid the bow, slid the paper from the box, and opened it—then inhaled the faint aroma of lavender and almond. She pulled the tissue paper away to reveal a bottle resting in a bed of red satin, the bottle being the source of the fragrance.

"Scentual massage oil," she said, reading the label before looking at Martin. "Got something on your mind?"

"Perhaps." He trailed his hand softly across her back. "But there's more in the box."

The "more" was a red satin negligee, accented with lace. She held it up, aware of how much it would *not* leave to the imagination.

"And I presume you want me to wear this?" she asked.

"You would look far better in it than I. After the kids are asleep."

"I see," she said, entertained by the idea but still suspicious of his reasons. "I'm still thinking you've done something you shouldn't have. You have that guilty look."

"Not at all. This is the season to give—a time for sharing and being closer with the one you love."

She snorted in disbelief. "Yeah, right. Now I know you've done something."

"Actually, I got the idea from the radio. Some preacher caused a big controversy by giving a sermon in favor of sex. Did you hear?" After she shook her head, he continued. "Well, this minister talked about how married couples can take each other for granted, not pay enough attention to each other, and so forth. This is why divorce is on the rise. He suggested that they start spending more time together in bed, because it's the time when they are the most connected."

A laugh slipped out of Bettye's mouth.

"You know what I mean," he said. "Sex brings couples closer together, physically, emotionally, and spiritually. At least, that is what he said. He proposed an intimacy diet of sorts: for ten days, every single night, couples plan on having sex."

Martin beamed as if he had won the lottery. "So, what do you think?"

"My, my, my," she said slowly while looking at the red naughty nightie. "I think you have some high expectations, considering our schedule. As it is, we do good to have sex every—"

Martin cleared his throat. "So think of it as a challenge with fringe benefits."

"Ten days straight is a long time."

"Twelve, actually," he corrected.

"I thought you said ten."

"The preacher said ten; however, I've taken some liberties. Since this is the holiday season and all, I thought we could do a 12 Days of Christmas kind of thing. I already have it planned out, with a lot of surprises along the way. There will be brightly wrapped holiday goodies, mistletoe, and decking the halls. We can even sing carols if you like. You're gonna love it. Think of it as the 12 Days of Sexmas!"

Bettye's eyes kept shifting from her husband to the negligee, and then to the oil, before she finally answered. "So how is this going to work?"

"Have you already forgotten?" he replied with a wicked grin.

"No, tonight."

"Well, our first task is to get the kids to bed. Then, while we wait for them to fall asleep, you can change into something more . . . comfortable. I can pour us some wine, have nice music in the background and candlelight to set the mood, and we can talk for a while."

"And then?"

"I open the oil and rub your back."

She smiled. "I'd like that."

"And your arms, then your legs, and then your feet. Then I can slowly move up and—"

"Oh, boy—presents!" came a voice from the doorway. Lizzie stood in her pajamas, hair still wet from her bath, with a gleam in her eyes. "Hey, Matt! Mommy and Daddy are opening presents!"

In a flash, Matt and Lizzie were on the bed with unbridled anticipation. "What is this?" she asked, pointing at the massage oil.

"Just something for Mommy," Martin answered, as Bettye covered the oil and negligee with the tissue.

"Where are ours?" they asked in harmony.

"Sorry. You have to wait until Christmas. This is a special treat for Mommy since she is so good to us. When you get to be a mommy, you can get one too."

"That's not fair," Matt said, "and I can't be a mommy. That's girl stuff."

"Then when you grow up, you can be the gift-giver."

"It's still not fair, and I want to open mine."

Lizzie seconded the vote. Bettye and Martin spent the next twenty minutes diffusing their expectations while ushering them through their nighttime ritual: brushing their teeth, bedtime stories, tucking them into bed, and wishing them the sweetest of dreams.

Through it all, Betty kept thinking of her favors on the bed and of the activities that awaited her. The more she thought of it, the more enticing the idea became, so that by the time she slipped into her new red nightie, she felt quite receptive to the possibilities.

As intimacies go, the evening was one of the most memorable she had in years.

—◦◦◦—

For Martin, this was more than just a way to reconnect. Once the idea occurred to him, he embraced the concept like a master architect, planning out each day in detail. It took full form following his visit to Lulu's Cabaret, a lingerie store that specialized in all things that happen behind closed doors. Shopping the Cabaret was akin to a child in a candy store, and Martin spent several hours examining all of their products.

The creative mind can be an unbridled thing if not held at bay, and for Martin, imagination ran amok as he wandered the aisles. Here, the possibilities were endless: clothing of all types, be it satin, lace, leather; from conventional dress to costumes, the latter including bunny suits and other woodland creatures, naughty nurses, fairies, devils, and dominatrix; condoms in various colors and textures; a full array of objects shaped like body parts, some battery operated, and with names like Power Viber, Rabbit Spread, Dreamer Teaser, Velveteen Jewel, and Mr. Squirmy; lotions, balms, and oils in different scents; magazines and books from steamy pictorials to how-to manuals on every possible theme and position; games of the card, board, and interactive variety; blow-up dolls of both sexes, jewelry, pumps, massagers, beads, rings, and other novelties. Some of the objects needed no explanation for their use; other devices appeared to be alien contraptions, whose purposes he could not even begin to guess.

The more he shopped, the more inventive his plan became. He made detailed notes on his phone, occasionally taking pictures, adding and rearranging items to a list of twelve. After weighing out his options, he picked the red lace nightie and massage oil as number one.

Bettye was going to have the time of her life. She just didn't know it yet.

After a well-spent afternoon, and with his wallet thinner, he left with several sacks full of a miscellany guaranteed to make a nun blush. Hell, even he blushed a bit.

—◊◊◊—

With day two came another gift, again left on the pillow, and a card with the inscription "No dusting until tonight." On top of it were two roses. Bettye was intrigued. The previous night's frolics had kept them up until two in the morning, well past Martin's normal bedtime and certainly past hers. Oh, but it had been romantic, and the idea of eleven more nights had its appeal.

She managed to get dinner pulled together well ahead of schedule. Then they worked in unison on the kids' bedtime ritual, and soon both Matt and Lizzie were dreaming of Christmas sugarplums and video games under the tree.

Once both children were safely out for the night, Martin and Bettye settled themselves on the bed.

"Dusting?" she asked after looking at the card. "I don't get it."

"You will in a minute."

The present turned out to be a decorative tin of honey powder along with a small feather duster.

She examined the can at all angles, searching for directions. "What is honey powder?"

"It's like powdering your nose, except you go for the whole body—and it's lickable."

"Ohhh . . ."

He added that the rose might be a feather substitute. While a novel idea, the duster worked quite well.

With day three came a trio of roses set on the bed beside a small, wrapped box and two candy canes. The offering was a card deck with silhouettes of couples in various positions on each card. The game appeared to be a hybrid of Strip Poker, Texas Hold 'Em, and Simon Says. It was far more entertaining than Bettye's weekly Bunko gatherings with the neighborhood wives. The candy canes made for some delightful, pepperminty smooches.

"Candy is dandy," he whispered in her ear, "but sex . . ." He didn't need to finish the line. She knew it already.

A second gift required no box; it played through the bedroom speakers after he downloaded it onto her phone music library: Ravel's *Bolero*.

"Wasn't this from a movie?" she asked.

"10."

"That's right. Marty, I'm afraid I may not have the figure of Bo Derek."

"Honey, Bo can't hold a candle to you."

—◦◦◦—

With day four, the reservations materialized. Yes, the evenings had been wonderful, even magical, yet also a bit sad since Bettye realized how little time she and Marty had spent together in recent years.

Worse, she felt damned tired in the mornings. She needed her solid eight hours of slumber, and three consecutive days of deprivation had its consequences. It took longer to get going, even requiring the additional cup of coffee she normally avoided.

And then there were the presents, which were starting to get more adventurous and, for lack of a better word, kinky. While she thought it all quite thoughtful, she was beginning to find herself out of her comfort zone. That became clear with the wrapped chocolate that evening, accompanying four red roses.

Of course, she loved chocolate of any size or type: milk, dark, or white. Martin knew this and would give her sweets for Valentine's Day, her birthday, Easter, and oftentimes for no particular reason. So being an unabashed chocolate junkie, she had no qualms about the substance. It had more to do with the usage.

It was a tube of edible chocolate body paint.

She realized that Marty might be developing a particular fixation on sex and food, but she decided not to press it. After insisting that towels cover her fine bed sheets, she consented, and all went deliciously well until she had been turned into a chocolate Van Gogh variation.

"Mommy?"

The voice scared the daylights out of both of them, sending the tube of paint flying across the room. Even as Bettye pulled up the bed sheets, Matt stood at the base of the bed looking like a wide-eyed-orphan painting.

"Mommy, I'm thirsty," he said.

After shooting eye darts at her husband for not closing the bedroom door, she reached for her robe and pulled it on, unsuccessfully attempting to hide the sugary evidence underneath. She merely managed to make more of a mess, now with chocolate smears all over the robe.

"Mommy, you have brown stuff on you."

"I spilled something," she replied as they walked to the kitchen. She fetched him a glass of water and walked him back to bed.

"That's chocolate, isn't it?" he asked.

"Yes, honey, it is." No point lying.

"Can I have some?"

"Maybe tomorrow. Go to sleep now." She tucked him in, leaving a stray candy smudge behind on the bed sheet. Matt closed his eyes and drifted off to slumber land.

Bettye marched downstairs with as much fire in her eyes as chocolate on her body. Martin had already put away the towels and changed the sheets, figuring that the confectionary part of the evening had come to an end.

"Why didn't you close the damned door?" she fumed. "Do you realize how awkward that was?"

She stood a few feet from him, an angry sight to behold, dressed in a white robe soiled with spots of brown, and her hair in disarray. Smudges of chocolate covered her face and stuck to a few stray locks of hair.

Martin attempted to keep a straight face, but that only lasted a few seconds. He fell to the bed, doubled over with laughter. Bettye was not amused, so she took the closest thing available—a pillow—and hurled it at him. For good measure, she took another pillow and began to pummel him with it. In defense, he did the same, and what began earlier as a contact sport with body paint ended as a traditional pillow fight.

They were up late again.

—ᴖᴠᴖ—

Martin made sure of two things the next night. First, that both kids were fast asleep, and second, to close and lock their door. As before, he resembled an eager puppy ready to play.

Five red roses lay on the pillow and were accented by golden costume jewelry rings on the stems.

"Five gold rings," Bettye mused. "So tomorrow I get six lords a-leaping? If they're male strippers, make sure they look like Jake Gyllenhaal."

"Sorry. It's a private party. Anyway, what's wrong with my dancing?"

Her grin contained an element of pity. "Honey, you don't dance; you shuffle."

Next to the flowers rested a single wrapped box, with the card bearing the inscription "Turn it on, turn *you* on." Inside, she found a battery-operated vibrating device. She examined it closely before commenting.

"I don't need you anymore," she told him.

Martin laughed at her joke, but somewhere deep down, he hoped she wasn't serious.

———

Night six was costume night.

Along with the six roses, there were three presents. The first two were large boxes. The card read "Open me first and dress for the occasion."

Inside the boxes were his and hers pirate costumes, hers being a "sexy Caribbean couture pirate," complete with leather, strappings, and lace. His was the standard "swashbuckler pirate," with an optional eye patch and a plush toy parrot attached to the shoulder.

She gave him a look of disbelief. "You must be fucking kidding."

"Avast, ye matey, don the suit or walk the plank," he answered in an absurd pirate voice.

"I am not putting this thing on."

"Come on, sweetheart. Use a little imagination. Picture this: We are in a large pirate boat in the middle of the ocean, the sea breeze licking at our faces, the Caribbean sun overhead. The ship is deserted, just you and me. We have charted a course for the nearest port, but it is still days away. All that time and nothing to do."

As he spoke, he began to massage her shoulders, always a weak point for her. She closed her eyes as she became one with the back rub, and her defenses began to topple. Then he threw in the clincher. "And there is buried treasure. To find it, you need the map." He leaned close to her ear, his breath tickling the lobe. "Let's get dressed."

Five minutes later, they were transformed into bedroom pirates. Bettye wore a skimpy black outfit with gloves and garters, accented by a large ornamental buckle belt and a pirate's hat. She felt ridiculous.

He thought she never looked sexier.

No self-respecting pirate would be caught dead in his costume, a poufy, open-shirt affair of brown and black fabrics, tied at the waist with a large belt and red sash. Another like-colored sash wrapped around his head, partially covered with a brown pirate's hat. What put the costume over the top was the combination of an eye patch and the misshapen parrot, which drooped from his shoulder at a forty-five-degree angle.

Bettye could no longer contain herself. "Do you really expect us to do it wearing these things?"

"Arrrrgh! We're going to do it pirate style," he answered, handing her a rolled sheet bound with ribbon.

She untied the ribbon, fingers fumbling due to the pirate gloves she wore, to find a pirate's map leading to the buried treasure. On a sheet of faux parchment, Martin had drawn a detailed layout of the bottom floor of their house in the shape of a deserted island, with a dotted line charting the course. There, on the other end of the island—the front room—was a large X, where lay the treasure.

She shook her head. "You have way too much time on your hands."

So began the grand adventure, leaving the good ship (their bed) and moving through the darkened house with lanterns (flashlights) in search of pirate's booty.

Naturally, they encountered a native on the island.

"Hi, Mommy. Hi, Daddy."

Matt stood before them in wonder, looking at each of them in turn. "Why are you dressed as Captain Jack?"

Since explaining sexual fantasies in pirate costumes didn't seem like a good idea, Bettye answered, "Honey, we were trying out new Halloween costumes."

"Can I play too?"

"No. You should be in bed."

"I'm thirsty."

"Again?" Bettye momentarily thought of running a garden hose to his room. "Let's get you some water."

"Can I wear my Spider-Man costume to bed?"

"I think that would be fine. But no mask," she instructed.

The two pirates took their son upstairs, let him change from pajamas to his Spidey suit from the previous Halloween, and took turns reading to him until he fell asleep. Rather than diminish the intended effect for the evening, it somehow made the experience all the more special. They sat on Matt's bed, looking at each other and at their little superhero, waiting until he fell asleep. Then, with flashlights at the ready, they made their way once more to where the X marked the spot, resting on the futon sofa.

The buried treasure turned out to be a bottle of spiced rum—the kind with the pirate on the label—along with a brandy glass to share. With the booty in hand, they made their way back to the soft confines of their ship, sampled the rum, the remainder of the evening, and each other.

From pirate to zombie, Bettye felt the blunt-force trauma lack of sleep by the morning of day seven. True, the evening before had been memorable—lovely in fact. She never in her wildest dreams could have pictured herself doing things like that, much less throwing herself wholeheartedly into the action, but on this morning, she felt like hell warmed over.

As usual, Martin bopped out the door for work, lively as ever. How he managed to get along with little sleep defied logic. After two full cups of coffee, Bettye felt little better, but only after a mid-afternoon nap did she get some energy back.

Martin followed up the pirate adventure with a movie night. The kids were shuffled off to bed even earlier than before, and when they were down for the count, Bettye put her seven roses in a vase with the others and unwrapped her gift.

She stared at a DVD with an obscene title, matching an equally obscene cover, along with a packet of microwave popcorn. They spent the evening watching XXX porn and munching on popcorn while sipping on the rum from the previous night. The movie was . . . educational, although he enjoyed it more than she did. Perhaps this was a guy thing, but she found it too explicit, preferring more left to the imagination. Still, one best learns by imitation, and a few new tricks were tried out that night.

More discoveries were to be made the following night—library night—with eight roses accompanying a lushly illustrated hardback edition of *Kama Sutra*. She had always heard of the classic text but had never read it. They leafed through the pages, read passages together, and decided on a suitable position. She thought the evening incredibly romantic, possibly because it did not require silly costumes or props, but it may have been the book lover in her.

Still, the daily toll had reached a breaking point, and the offering on day nine confirmed that a change was necessary. She hadn't a clue what the object was: a set of plastic balls attached by a string, rather like an oversized set of beads. When Martin explained what they were used for, she told him where he could stick them. She opted instead for simplicity, missionary, and without oils, lubes, edible material, or costumes—and certainly without beads.

This twelve-day scheme was typical of Martin, who constantly came up with hair-brained ideas, only a few of which turned out to be good. More times than not, they were idiotic. She still winced at the memories of the holographic Christmas tree he had bought several years earlier, which conjured up as much holiday cheer as a stocking full of coal. He thought it quite clever and high-tech. She thought it horrid and finally pulled the plug on the ghastly thing.

The time had come for decisive action. By the next morning, and with a firm resolve, she set a new plan into motion. As much as she loved Martin—and yes, she had enjoyed the last nine days—well, a girl's gotta do what a girl's gotta do.

So on a cool December morning, well into the second week of their holiday sexathon, Bettye made her first trip to Lulu's Cabaret. There she wandered the aisles, but unlike her husband, she felt a combination of shocked dismay and fascination. She had no idea of the sundry things people could do to each other—or themselves. At last, she found what she wanted, made her purchase, and left.

That evening, Bettye stood ready and dressed in the negligee Martin had given her on the very first night.

"Wow," Martin said, looking her over from top to bottom. She had never looked lovelier.

When he slid a wrapped package across the bed along with the nine roses, she read the attached card: "So smooth against the skin."

"Whatever can it be?" she asked. She removed the ribbon and lifted the lid. Inside, she found a set of pastel-pink satin bed sheets.

"My, what a *practical* gift."

"I thought you would like it." Martin moved in for his first kiss of the evening, but she placed her hand on his chest.

"I have something special of my own planned for tonight," she countered.

She led him by the hand into the living room, with the mood already set. Lights had been dimmed, the fireplace blazed with a gentle warmth, and soft music filled the background. There upon the futon frame sofa sat a gift bag, hers for him, tied with a neat bow, and a card addressed simply "To Martin, with love from Bettye." He sat on the sofa and opened the bag. Beneath layers of tissue, he found a set of red handcuffs, with the inner rings lined with soft red fur.

"I thought we might try some *restraint* tonight," she said seductively.

She slid up to him, caressed his chest, and quickly got him into the spirit of the moment. Yet each time he tried to move his hands underneath her negligee, she pulled them back, eventually stretching his arms up above his head. Then she straddled him, still holding his hands at bay, and asked demurely, "Are you ready?"

"I've never done anything like this before."

"There's always a first time," she purred. She took the handcuffs, gently wrapped each one around his wrists, and clicked them shut, making sure each was just tight enough but without discomfort. Then she connected the other ends to the wooden posts on the sofa.

She moved her torso back and forth on top of him and whispered in his ear, "Are you hot?"

"Oh, yes," he moaned.

"And you want me badly?"

"Yes. More than ever," he moaned.

"And how long can you wait?"

"For you, anything."

She smiled. Then she rose to her feet, stretching her arms out to either side. "I'm really tired," she announced. "I'm going to bed."

It took several seconds for Martin to comprehend the game change. "But . . . but . . ."

At the doorway, she turned. "A woman needs a little down time."

"You can't leave me like this . . . can you? What if the kids come down?"

"Darling, you'll think of something. You have all night." She blew him a kiss. "Good night, sweetheart. And thanks for the sheets. I think they're wonderful."

With that, Bettye strolled to their bedroom for a good night of well-deserved and uninterrupted sleep.

SEX AND THE FAT GIRL

Sue Roman

A FRIEND TOLD PATTY that she knew someone who was perfect for her. She'd heard it before, but this time she believed this friend and it made her curious. She was almost twenty-five years old and hadn't found the perfect man yet. She'd spread her legs for a few hopeful candidates in college, but none was "perfect." Patty was a fat girl. It was the 1970s, and because of how she looked she usually got the leftovers: the guys who by today's standards were geeks or losers. Back then she didn't think she deserved anyone better than who she managed to get. Then her friend called to tell her about someone she thought Patty should meet. Unfortunately, she also told Patty that the guy was recently separated from his wife. Not Patty's first choice, but why the hell not? She wasn't looking for forever. She was having a long dry spell, and it might be fun.

Some time passed before they actually met. In fact, Patty had almost forgotten about him, but then one day her friend called and invited her to a party. The guy, Bill, was going to be there. The party was at someone's house Patty didn't know. She didn't like parties like that, but Bill would be there so she had to go.

When she walked in, Patty scanned the room and her eyes landed on a guy in the middle of the room surrounded by several people. She hoped this was Bill, and when her friend told her it was Patty let out a sigh of relief. She recognized his type immediately. He was the guy everyone wanted to be around. The women were fawning all over him, and men handed him beer. Bill *was* the party.

He was about 5'8" with reddish-blond hair. A short, thick, reddish-colored beard framed his face. Even from across the room, Patty could tell he had great sparkling eyes. He had a huge barrel chest, and from what she could see, he was all muscle. He had the most wonderful laugh, which filled the room when something or someone amused him. He laughed a lot during the party. Everything about him screamed "bad boy," but what woman in her right mind didn't want to be involved with a bad boy at least once in her life? After watching him for a while, Patty convinced herself that maybe her friend was right: maybe he would be perfect for her, but she knew she would never be perfect for him. He seduced almost every woman at the party. He laughed and listened intently when he talked to them, and he would lightly touch a shoulder, leaning in to hear what they had to say. He was good at this. It wouldn't be hard for him to choose any woman there. She liked watching him work the room; it was amazing. Why in the world would he want her?

Patty's friend eventually came back over to her and grabbed her hand. They walked over to Bill together. He was cordial and smiled that smile, instantly seducing her into believing she was his new best friend. She was hooked, and more importantly, she wanted him and it didn't matter if he didn't want her. She tried to talk to him, but he was surrounded by people. After they were introduced, he nodded and then turned back to the group he'd been talking with. After a while, Patty gave up trying to get his attention, walked across the room, and went back to watching.

She made her play about an hour later. She'd had a couple of drinks by then so was fully charged and ready to attack. She knew all the right moves because she'd been at this seduction thing for a long time. She'd been to enough college parties to know the rules and, more importantly, knew how to seduce. Ninety percent of the time that was the only way she could get laid.

She moved in for the kill: She snuggled up to him, told him her name again just in case he'd forgotten it, and then told him that their mutual friend said they should meet because they had a lot in common. He looked at her for a hard second. "That's nice," Bill replied, and he walked away.

What just happened? Whatever happened wasn't supposed to happen. She'd seduced college men, goddammit! Who was this guy? He was just some plumber whose wife left him, that's who. He was rude, and she was pissed. He'd talked to every bitch at the party, laughed with them, and cooed them, and all he gave Patty was one second of his precious time. What an asshole. Who needed him? She sure as hell didn't. Fuck him!

Patty walked back across the room to nurse her bruised ego and grabbed a handful of Jell-O shots to ease the pain.

It was getting late, and just about everyone had left; the pickings were slim. She glanced around, and all that was left was Bill talking to the host and hostess, a couple necking on the sofa, three guys draining the last of a keg, a woman passed out in a chair, and Patty. His choice came down to Patty and the woman passed out in the chair.

She pulled herself together, slurped down the last Jell-O shot, walked over to where he stood near the food table, and tried again. The old second-time's-the-charm trick. As she got closer to him, she could smell his maleness, and it was intoxicating: he was dripping pheromones, and it filled her senses.

This time she snuggled in much closer. She placed her crotch to just slightly touch his hip. Let's see if he'd ignore her now.

Bill pulled himself away and jammed his hand between her legs. It took her breath away. No one had ever done that before.

They were face to face, and she could feel his chest rise and fall with every breath he took. She was in the hunt, and even with a fire building between her legs, she knew from experience that at this exact moment she had to appear cool and in complete control. There would be plenty of time to fall apart later.

"It's too late to get a motel. Where do you live?" he asked.

"Just follow me. I'm parked down the block a little way from here."

"Lead on."

She'd done it: She stayed cool during their brief encounter. It wasn't easy; every inch of her was on fire. Patty closed her eyes, and for a second she smiled to herself. She was elated; she'd won the door prize and had seduced the most wanted guy in the room. Yay, Patty! No way was she going to allow herself to think that the only reason she'd won was because she was the only one left standing.

He pulled his hand out of her crotch and followed her home.

Patty lived with her sister in a house they couldn't afford. It was a nice little house with two bedrooms. Most nights Patty spent them alone in her room, but tonight she was going to have company. She wouldn't be alone—not tonight. She was sure her sister would hear them when they came in, but she didn't care. She was going to have sex. Her sister would have to get over it. But when Patty looked in her sister's room, it was empty. Good.

The only light coming into her room was from a living-room lamp. That left it just dark enough that her completely out-of-shape body wouldn't kill the mood when he saw her naked.

"Turn on a light. I don't do this with the lights off; I want to see you," he ordered.

"Shit." She grabbed her shirt and pulled it down as far as she could to cover her hips.

Bill grabbed her shoulder and turned her face to his. He leaned in and whispered into her ear, "I don't care what you look like. I want to see your face while I fuck you."

She knew she blushed and was glad it was just dark enough that he couldn't see it. She reached down to turn on a bedside light and started to undress.

She was completely naked in about ten seconds. He took his time, and she sat down to watch. Patty was right: He was a lot of muscle wrapped around a short frame. He had a nasty-looking scar that wrapped its way from just under his left ribcage down to his hip, and it looked like he'd had it for a long time. It was the only mar she could see on him. And much to her joy, he had a hairy chest, and the hair was the same color blond as on his head. What a lucky girl she was.

Patty crawled into the center of the bed, taking her usual missionary position. She raised herself to her elbows and waited for him. He turned his back and finally pulled off his shorts. He had the best-looking ass she'd ever seen, and she could only hope when he turned around he would reveal the grand prize.

She wasn't at all disappointed. He was magnificent. She'd never seen such a fine, huge display of junk in her life.

Now that the strip show was over, he didn't waste any time. He crawled on top of her and threw open her legs. Before she knew it, his penis was lightly pressing her closed labia. Then he stopped.

"Goddammit, open your eyes!" he demanded.

"Sorry."

He moved up higher on her chest, repositioned his penis, and then started the dance. He pushed himself in a little way and then pulled out; pushed in again a little farther and then pulled out again, but not quite all the way. He wasn't even inside her yet, and she was ready to explode.

"You're killing me. Get inside me, quick!" *Oh my God*, Patty thought to herself. Maybe this time, maybe this time she'd actually have an orgasm. If this is what passion felt like, it was good.

He pushed in again but this time didn't pull out. He rocked inside her, and when Patty was writhing in pleasure he went in for the kill. He rammed into her, paused, and began ever so slowly and rhythmically to rock inside her. She couldn't think; she couldn't focus. There was no Patty; there was no Bill—only what was happening between her legs and nothing else. He stopped again, pulled himself out, and then leaned down and kissed her forehead. Without saying a word, he grabbed her left leg and pulled it as far over her chest as he could get it. Then he did the same with her right leg. He pulled her hips down, and when she looked down all she could see was her black tuft of pubic hair vertical to the ceiling. He grabbed the pillow on either side of her head and rammed himself inside again. This time he pummeled her insides and she could only feel exquisite pain mixed with unbelievable pleasure. A few seconds later he closed his eyes, threw his head back, and exploded inside her. She felt his penis spilling out semen in a flood inside her. She felt every pulse. This is what she'd been missing; this is what she was looking for. This guy was the perfect lover, and the scream her body made when he came inside her was everything. Patty had finally discovered the orgasm.

He rolled off her and wiped himself off with a sheet. He laid back down, putting a space between them, placed the back of his hand on Patty's breast, took a couple of deep breaths, and fell asleep.

It was the best sex she'd ever had. She didn't care that he'd fallen asleep; he'd worked hard and was completely spent, and so was Patty. Only Patty didn't sleep. She never did after sex. She'd sleep after he left; there would be plenty of time for sleep when she was alone again.

He had totally ruined her, and she didn't give a shit. He was the only man she'd ever want inside her again.

Sometime during the night, her sister came in. She tapped on Patty's door and opened it slightly.

"You all right?"

"I have someone with me," Patty answered. "I'll tell you about it in the morning. Night."

"Night."

Bill suddenly roused and sat up. "I gotta go." He dressed. Patty threw on her t-shirt and walked him out to his truck.

"Am I going to see you again?"

"Sure. Why not?" he replied casually.

"When we were at the party, I slipped my number into your shirt pocket."

"Great." He touched her left breast and without another word, turned, walked to his truck, and left.

She stood there in the cool, early morning breeze watching as his headlights disappeared around the corner. She waited. Maybe he'd change his mind and come back. A few minutes passed. A cat startled her when it came out from under a car, trotted across the street, and disappeared into a hedge. She realized all she had on was a t-shirt and that she was standing in her driveway staring down the street into darkness.

She turned and went back into the house, turned off the living room light, and walked back into her room. It smelled of sex and beer. The sheets were wet, but she didn't care. She stripped the bed, pulled off her t-shirt, grabbed a blanket off the floor, and fell fast asleep.

She spent the next day waiting for a call that never came. It didn't come the next day, either, or the day after that. In fact, it was almost a week before the call finally came. It was 2:30 in the morning. She was pissed, but like every woman in her right mind, when you are exposed to nirvana, you want that exposure again and as much as possible at whatever time it's offered. She answered the phone on the third ring.

"Hello."

"You home?" Bill asked.

"Of course I'm home. You called me at home, didn't you?"

"Oh, yeah. Can I come over?"

"It's the middle of the night, and I can tell you're drunk." She wasn't going to cut him any slack, damn it. She had a bruised ego to think about, damn it.

"Can I come over or not?" he repeated.

"OK, but be quiet. My sister is home." So much for her principles.

"Maybe she'd like to join us." He laughed that laugh, goddamn him.

"Fuck you!" she exclaimed.

"Exactly." He hung up.

For some stupid reason, she waited and watched out the bay window in the living room for him. An hour later, he finally pulled into the driveway. She walked out to meet him, and even from three feet away he reeked of cigarette smoke, stale beer, and sweat. It was disgusting.

It didn't take much for him to figure out she was pissed, so as they walked into the house he put his hand on her waist. Once inside he pulled her to him and kissed her. Not a tongue-down-the-throat kind of kiss but the kind of kiss that could make toes curl and knees go weak. It was the first time he'd kissed her on the mouth.

When they got into the hallway that separated Patty's bedroom from her sister's, he stopped.

"You sure your sister won't want to join us?" he asked.

"Fuck you."

"OK, lead the way." He chuckled then lightly slapped her butt.

She turned on the light, and much the same way as the first time, he finished undressing after she did. He gave her another great view of his nakedness and then crawled in beside her.

"Look, I'm sorry it's late. My crew and I were up in the Woodlands, and we got back late."

"Oh." She wanted to stay cool, but the fire was building.

His finger slowly circled her breast. "Then someone wanted to go to Mac's bar and, well one thing lead to another and . . ."

"And you felt obligated to go."

"Do you want to fuck or not?" Obviously he wasn't going to put up with her attitude.

She pulled off her t-shirt, and before she could lie back down, he was on her. This time he didn't play "May I come in?" He spread open her legs, stuck a finger up her vagina, and when he was satisfied that it was wet enough, pushed himself inside. She didn't care—she had him where he wanted to be, and nothing else mattered. He folded her in half again and rammed himself home. She whimpered a bit because the force of him ramming inside her hurt, but the pain didn't last long. Isn't that what sex is about: pleasure mixed with pain mixed with ecstasy? Pleasure trumped pain. Being folded in half for his pleasure was worth it, wasn't it?

Before Bill she'd only known mediocrity. Those fumbling men in college were as uneducated and unskilled in sexual technique as she was. This man knew what he was doing and did it really, really well.

They met like this a few more times, and each time it was the same. He'd call in the middle of the night, and when he'd finally show up she'd act pissed. Then he'd fly her to the moon.

This kept on for a while. At some point Patty grew tired of the booty calls. The thrill was gone. Passion isn't a one-way thing. She hadn't felt it in a while, and she realized that she'd never seen it in his eyes. When the frequency of his late-night calls grew to weeks, it was time for her to move on.

Patty hooked up with PJ next. He was from New York. A New York Jew, short and well-endowed, he had curly black hair all over his body.

He was the complete opposite of Bill in every way. His method was so different. Bill had the slam-bang blow-out-your-brains technique, where PJ was tender. His pre-coital was heaven. He loved to kiss, loved to cuddle, and he took all the time in the world to make sure she was ready before he climbed on top of her. Being with PJ was like a slow and fluid dance: He slipped inside her and when he felt she was ready, he slammed her up against the headboard and drove himself home. Just before he climaxed, he pulled himself almost out of her, took a deep breath, and hit the slammer again. Patty didn't know whether to laugh or cry. All she knew was that she wanted more of him, and PJ certainly delivered. When he finally exploded, she felt her hips rise and fall and she completely disappeared. Even after he rolled off her, it still felt like he was inside her. She throbbed and it felt so damn good.

For a long time Patty was sure that Bill had ruined her for other men, but maybe PJ had ruined her for Bill.

PJ stayed the night. They had breakfast with her sister, and later that morning he left with a promise to call.

That afternoon he called and invited Patty to dinner and said he'd cook. What? Great sex and he cooks too? Oh, gawd!

He lived in a big house that had been converted into six apartments. His place was on the first floor, and it looked like him. It was quirky: colored scarves draped the lamps, mismatched rugs covered the floors, movie posters covered the walls, and a Smith Corona typewriter sat on the end of a small table and had a piece of typed paper resting under the paper bail. The bed was a full-size mattress on the floor. PJ was a hippie, and from the looks of his world he would probably stay one.

True to his word, he fixed dinner. A small broiled steak with green beans, a salad, and wine with a cork. He was a good cook. After dinner, they listened to records and she let him talk politics. Nixon was in the White House, and the Vietnam War was raging. He told her he wanted to be a journalist. He liked to talk, so Patty listened. She had no opinion to share. Any opinion she had was black and white. Patty hated Nixon and detested the war. She'd lost high school friends in that war. She stayed out of discussions about either topic because her opinion had no sides, but she was a good listener. She knew how to move her head in a way that was in neither agreement nor disagreement. The method satisfied most people because it allowed them to keep talking.

Patty spent the night with PJ, wrapped in his arms on the mattress on the floor. Earlier he'd lit several candles, and incense filled the air with the woodsy smell of patchouli. And, like the night before, he romanced her for a long time before he owned her again.

She really liked him. He was so not like anyone she'd ever known before. He was quirky in a good sort of way, knew what he wanted out of life and they just clicked.

She liked being romanced. She liked the way he kissed her. It was not the kind of kiss some men do as a precursor to sex; it was a passionate "I'm glad to be here with you" kind of kiss. She liked the way he caressed her and made her feel wanted and, more particularly, desired. Patty knew in her heart that he really wanted to be with her. Maybe he was the perfect guy for her. Maybe.

They slept together almost every night for a few more weeks, and then out of the blue he had a call from his hometown newspaper offering him a job as a cub reporter. Before she knew it, he had packed up all the lovely scarves, rolled up the rugs, tapped out the incense, and blew out the candles. He was gone within a week, and she never heard from him again.

Was this the way it was going to be? She'd meet someone, and within a few weeks or a couple of months they'd be gone? Was this her curse? She'd opened her heart, allowed herself to feel happy, and in the blink of an eye it was gone.

She stayed celibate for a long time after that. She hadn't heard from Bill in months. Her friend told her he'd gone back to his wife. The wife threw him out because two women had filed paternity suits against him. His freewheeling dick had gotten him into trouble. The wife would take him back on the condition he'd get himself snipped. He did, so she took him back. Now Patty knew why he hadn't called. Shit.

Life as she knew it returned to normal, whatever that was.

She threw herself into work, and one night at a party she met some people who wanted to start a community theater. There was a well-established one in town, but it had gotten so cliquish that anyone new was never allowed to do anything but build sets and make costumes. The people at the party wanted to change that. Patty had a degree in theater and, more importantly, had a full time job that paid good money, so she joined the group as sometime director, all the time producer, and chief wrangler of actors and procurer of potential members.

After a few successful productions, they posted an open call looking for someone to direct a two-woman play. The open call brought Bill back.

Shortly after rehearsals began and in the middle of the night, Patty's phone rang. It was him.

"You home?"

"Who is this?" She knew but pretended she didn't.

"It's Bill. Can I come over?"

"I thought you were back with your wife. How'd the paternity suits turn out?"

"I miss you. I want to see you. Can I come over?" he repeated

"I haven't heard from you in months, you call in the middle of the night, and I'm supposed to welcome you with open arms—or should I say open legs?"

"The open legs work. Can. I. Come. Over. Pleasssse?"

"I guess."

What was wrong with her? She was tired of the booty calls; she wanted wooed, wanted flowers, wanted to be dated, and wanted to be seen in the light of day with the man she was having sex with. Why was she always settling for middle-of-the-night, ball-busting sex? Because fuck it—she loved the sex and missed it. In fact, it's the only thing she missed about Bill. She missed his great, big engorged penis slamming into her backbone.

She'd had great sex with PJ, but sooner or later she knew she'd grow tired of his soft music and incense and hour-long sexcapades. Who was she kidding—she wanted down and dirty "thank you for fucking me" sex, and Bill's penis was just the thing to do that.

When he knocked on the door, she let him in but didn't talk to him. She led him into the bedroom closed the door and stripped off her clothes. He waited for her. He started to undress, but Patty reached over, unzipped his pants, and pulled down his shorts. She tipped him back onto the bed, crawled up between his legs, and sucked his dick down her throat. It took him completely by surprise, and from the look on his face, he liked it. Then she put her tongue to work. She felt the ridge that separated the head of his penis from the shaft and slowly swirled her tongue around it. She felt the tiny scar from his circumcision and ran her tongue up and down it.

Afterward she made a slow and deliberate circle with her tongue around his penis's head, Patty pushed her mouth down farther and then slowly moved her mouth up and down his shaft. The soft moans coming from him meant she was doing a good job. With the first taste of the sour acidic fluid seeping from the head, she pulled her mouth off him and rolled him on top of her. He was about ready to explode when she had him in her mouth, so it didn't take long for him to erupt inside her. There was no passion between them: just sex.

He would remember tonight, and he'd be back. Patty made sure of that.

"You've killed me," he said.

"Good."

Maybe the fat girl was perfect for him after all.

❧ NO INHIBITION ☙

Andrya Bailey

"*LAST TANGO IN PARIS*," Isabelle heard a husky, sexy voice whisper over her shoulder. "Have you ever watched it?"

She was startled when the man sat at her table unceremoniously and uninvited. His smoldering smile made her blush, and his piercing, smoky green eyes were locked on hers. He was tall and tan, with tousled ash-blond hair, and wearing a pair of ripped jeans and a button-down white shirt with the sleeves rolled up, showing muscular, strong arms. He was definitely the most striking man she had ever set her eyes on. She had been sitting at the coffee shop by herself for the last half hour, enjoying the pleasant afternoon in Paris, sipping a now-cold cappuccino. Her flight back to New York was the following day, and she was contemplating how to spend the rest of her last day in the romantic city.

"Excuse me?" she asked in a barely audible voice. His hypnotizing eyes made her quiver. What kind of effect did this stranger exert that her voice could hardly be heard?

"*Last Tango in Paris*," he repeated in a light accent. "The agency got it right this time. You really look a lot like the actress in the movie. Perfect! You'll be a great subject for the project. I'm having great ideas already. You've watched it, haven't you?"

Isabelle stared at him, shaking her head in confusion. "Yes, I've . . . watched it." She could feel the blood rushing to her face as she remembered the infamous butter scene of Bertolucci's polemic '70s film. What was she doing talking about this movie with a seducing stranger? She cleared her throat. "I think you're confusing me with someone else. Or is this your cheesy pick-up line?"

The sexy man frowned, but his tantalizing smile didn't fade from his handsome, tanned face. Isabelle was mesmerized by him, and deep inside she was hoping he was indeed using a cheesy pick-up line on her.

"Don't tell me—you're not my American model? I'm so sorry." He took his eyes off her for a minute to scan the other tables around, shaking his head. Then he pulled his cell phone out of his shirt pocket, checked it, typed something quickly, and put it back. "I was late for the meeting, and she didn't wait. Not interested enough, I guess. But you're just perfect. I doubt she would be any prettier than you in person." His enticing eyes were on her again.

"Thanks," she mumbled, trying to avoid his stare.

"You are so beautiful! You could take her place. What are your plans?" He leaned forward, placing his elbow on the table to rest his chin on his hand. His gaze made her heart skip a beat.

"My plans?"

"Yes. Are you free today? For the rest of the afternoon, or for the rest of the night, maybe?" He grinned.

"To do what?" She wondered what he had in mind. What a way to end her weeklong vacation if she were to spend the rest of the day with this sexy stranger.

"To play *Last Tango in Paris*: my version."

His smoky voice made her tremble. Isabelle suddenly felt a burning desire in her groin. Did he mean having sex like in *Last Tango in Paris*? Was this what he was really suggesting? Her dark fantasy of being seduced by a stranger was taking shape in her mind. Yes, this guy could make it real. She probably wouldn't even think twice, and for once in her life she could act naughty: have a one-night stand the way she secretly dreamed. Her last night in Paris.

She gaped at him. "What do you mean?"

"What do you think of the movie?" He leaned back on the chair and crossed his muscular arms across his well-toned chest, observing her intently. Her eyes feasted on his body.

"Well, two strangers met in Paris and had a torrid affair without knowing anything about each other, not even their names. What do I think of it? Nothing short of erotic and somewhat perverted," she managed to say in a quiet voice, wondering if that's what he was thinking about.

He winked seductively. "I'm an artist. I was commissioned to paint a scene from the movie, but my model just bailed out . . . and you look gorgeous."

"Oh, no, I've never modeled before." Isabelle tried to conceal her disappointment and shook her head in disbelief from her own mischievous thoughts. He wanted to paint her, not fuck her, of course. The fantasy would remain a fantasy—in her dreams.

"You just stand there. I do the rest. It's that easy!"

"It's my last day in Paris. I'm flying back to New York tomorrow. I don't think there's enough time for you to paint me in one afternoon. And I don't even know you."

He cocked his head and waved his hands sensually, as if he was painting an invisible canvas. "You'd be surprised at what I can do with my brushes and my hands."

Isabelle bit her lip. Her heart was beating fast. "How do you play your version of *Last Tango*?"

He leaned forward again, and his hand reached across the table. His fingers curled under her chin to gently lift her face. Bouts of electric tension ran down her spine upon his touch. "If you're curious, I can show you how I play my version of *Last Tango*. Come to my studio with me; it's not far from here," he said with a commanding and firm tone, making him even more enthralling.

"I don't even know who you are," she attempted to protest.

"I'm convinced it was no coincidence that you were here today instead of my model. It is what it is. I'm the one you'll spend your last day in Paris with. Isn't that enough for you to know?" His intense stare made her feel naked. She was irresistibly drawn to him.

"Can you at least tell me your name?" Isabelle asked as the attractive Frenchman stood up, inviting her to follow him.

He reached out for her hand. "It's *Last Tango*, ma chèrie. No names. Come."

What a way to spend her last day of vacation! She was accepting to go to a stranger's home to model for an erotic painting and perhaps experience an impetuous sexual adventure. No coincidence, he had said. It was fate. She wouldn't fight this burning, inexplicable lust. She gave him her hand and he took it to his full, plump lips, planting a moist kiss on her that sent shivers down her back. All she could do was to nod in agreement, unable to resist the mysterious foreigner.

They walked hand in hand through the streets of Paris until they reached a brick-built, low-rise building shaded by blooming chestnut trees. He unlocked the door to the first floor, and they entered a loft that really looked like an art studio. There were canvases, easels, paintbrushes, and tools all over the place. Splatters of paint dotted the floor, while drawings, sketches, and paintings hung around every available inch on the walls. At a darker and cleaner corner stood an inviting four-post king-size bed covered in red silk sheets and pillows. Isabelle bit her lower lip, fantasizing about being taken by him in this tempting red-hot bed.

He released her hand and walked toward a small cooler sitting on top of a sink buried with cans and tubes of paint and paintbrushes. Isabelle studied the place, admiring the work of the artist. All the paintings depicted beautiful nude or semi-nude women in erotic, sensual, inviting poses. She was immediately aroused by the seductive scenario. She wanted him to fuck her. Maybe he fucked all the women who modeled for him. Yes, she could do that. It was her last night in the city, and she would let herself be seduced by an unknown French artist. What could be sexier than that? No coincidence. He came back bringing two glasses of red wine and handed her one.

"To your last night in Paris," he said before taking a sip of the velvety liquid. Isabelle gulped her wine at once, enthralled by his hypnotizing green eyes.

"Do you really want me to model for you?" she asked on impulse.

He took the empty glass from her hand, and his tempting smile spread across his face. "Yes, I want to paint you if you pose for me. And I also want to see and feel your sensual body squirming under my brush strokes. It's your last night, isn't it? Let me satisfy your innermost desires."

Her tongue inadvertently swiped across her lips, and she looked at him from head to toe, imagining his toned and chiseled body on top of her. She never lusted for someone like this before. It didn't take long for her to feel the dizzying effect of the wine rushing to her head.

"Surprise me with your version of *Last Tango*, then," she said demurely.

"My version. No inhibition." He tilted his head and touched her face lightly with the back of his hand, waiting for her consent.

Isabelle nodded, closing her eyes and exhaling a deep breath. "No inhibition," she whispered in a trembling voice, savoring his touch on her tingling skin. She imagined how it would feel to have him inside of her.

He put the glasses away, picked up a large easel, placed it at a small distance from the bed, arranged an empty canvas on it, and spread several tubes of paint and brushes on the floor next to it. Once his workspace was set, he walked slowly toward her, gazing at her with his intense stare. Her heart was beating fast; the thought of posing for him was arousing her deeply. He put his hands around her. Reaching behind her, he slowly unzipped her dress. His face was so close to hers that she thought he was going to kiss her. She could smell his musky, masculine scent, and the touch of his fingers on her skin ignited a wet flow between her legs. She breathed deeply and closed her eyes as her dress slid easily to the floor, and she became aware she was wearing only her silky black lingerie.

"Beautiful," she heard his raspy voice say. "You are alluring."

Isabelle opened her eyes to find him looking at her with hungry eyes. When he picked her up and carried her to the large bed, she locked her arms around his neck, enjoying the sudden intimacy. He placed her gently on the soft, fragrant sheets. She was so smitten by the sexy stranger that she was almost out of breath.

"Lie down on the pillows, place your arms next to your body like this, and put this leg over the other," he instructed as he touched each of the body parts he wanted to arrange for the perfect pose. At each brush of his strong hands on her skin, she felt goosebumps and couldn't help feeling the sexual intensity growing inside of her. She wanted him to forget about the painting and get in bed with her, but instead she allowed him to manipulate her body into the ideal position. How long would she be able to endure this?

"Perfect," he said, taking a long, sensual look at her carefully laid body. "Now just stay like this, and give me the sexiest look you can. Look at me as if you really want me to forget about the painting and have passionate, raw, crazy sex like in *Last Tango in Paris* with you right now."

She blinked and pouted, trying her most seductive look on him. "Not hard to do that," she mumbled.

He raised his eyebrows and smirked, leaving Isabelle in her seductive pose. He turned on a small CD player that lay on a three-foot stool next to the bed. As Bowie's romantic and poignant "Absolute Beginners" started to play, he took his position in front of the easel.

Isabelle didn't move. She lay there trying to wow him with her lustful stare, imagining his hands all over her while she watched his eyes moving frantically between her and the canvas as he ferociously worked with a piece of charcoal to make a sketch.

After what seemed an eternity, he sighed, put the tools back on the floor, and wiped the thin line of sweat that had formed on his forehead with the back of his hand. He looked sexier than ever. She felt his eyes piercing hers with a wild desire. He walked to the other side of the loft where the cooler was and filled the glasses with wine again.

"You can rest for now." He handed her one of the glasses. After drinking his, he slowly unbuttoned his shirt to reveal his spectacularly toned abs, square shoulders, and muscled arms. Again, she drank the glass of wine in one gulp, admiring the perfectly chiseled sculpture in front of her. He removed his jeans and threw them on the floor, making her gasp when she saw how magnificently hard he was. Isabelle longed to touch him.

He climbed in bed on top of her. "You were really looking at me as if you wanted me to forget about the painting and have passionate, raw, crazy sex like in *Last Tango in Paris* with you. It was hard concentrating." He bit her upper lip lightly while swiftly unhooking her bra and tossing it on the floor. His eyes paused on her plump, already swollen breasts, and he kissed her with passion before raising both her arms over her head to handcuff her. Isabelle gasped. He paused for a second and looked deep in her eyes. "Is this what you want? For me to have passionate, raw, crazy sex like in *Last Tango in Paris* with you—my version? No inhibition?"

"No inhibition," she murmured. "That's what I want. Your version."

"You are so beautiful," he whispered in her ear and blindfolded her with a sleeping mask before slipping his hands under her panties to tear them off. He put his fingers in between her legs. "And you're so ready," he said, pleased to feel her moisture.

Opening her legs wide, he tied her ankles to her tights with silk ribbons to have her pussy completely open, exposed to him. Isabelle moaned. Her heart was racing, and she had no idea what to expect, but this stranger was much better than she had ever imagined in her dark, secret sexual fantasies. She couldn't wait to feel him hard and throbbing inside her.

His probing fingers opened her to explore each corner and each fold of skin underneath. She let out a loud sigh when his hands moved to caress every inch of her body. He licked and sucked her nipples slowly with a fierce grip of his lips while she wriggled under him, begging to be released. He went down on her with his tongue and his lips, but before she could reach her ecstasy, he stopped the teasing and lifted her bottom.

"I don't have butter," he said, referring to the movie's most harrowing scene. Isabelle's heart pounded hard as she knew what was coming and she shook her head, enveloped by the darkness of the blindfold mask.

"Oh . . ." she murmured, feeling a warm, greasy liquid being poured on her.

"I have something better: chocolate-flavored body oil. With a condom," she heard him whisper.

Suddenly she was aware of his aching, throbbing penis penetrating her ass and fucking her hard while she was all bound and tied to his liking. Her fingers curled into a tight fist while she gritted her teeth in painful pleasure. His movements were precise and rhythmical, and he slid in easily inside her with the help of the oil. It didn't take long for him to reach his climax, and she heard him uttering a satisfying growl as he removed his thick, long penis out of her.

She heard him panting as he untied her legs and stretched them out on the bed. A sensual warmth enveloped her skin, as she felt the oil being poured on her breasts. He massaged the oil slowly on her nipples, rubbing, pulling, and teasing them between his fingers, rolling and raising them until they were as big and hard as two marbles. Making his way down with his skilled hands, he lightly caressed her chest, navel, and crotch before opening her legs again to reveal her moist vagina. Then he rubbed some oil on her swollen clit.

The tension in her was building again. As Isabelle let out a loud groan, he moved down to rub and massage her legs, her calves, her ankles, her feet, and her toes, preventing her from reaching her ecstasy. Torturing her while she moaned with desire, his tongue and lips trailed slowly up her legs, savoring the flavored oil, lick by lick, until she felt him touch her dripping pussy. He licked the oil and juice off of her fiercely, working with his tongue back and forth, in and out, lavishing in her movements as she raised her hips and body in anticipation of the coming orgasm. She exploded in a loud scream as she finally reached her ecstasy, shivering with indescribable pleasure as wave after wave of sexual rapture washed over her body. Her heart pounded so hard inside her chest, she thought it was going to burst. She was almost out of breath. She had never reached such an agonizingly powerful release before. He was not finished. While she was still visibly shaken and trying to recover from her violent orgasm, he gently moved her out of the bed and got her on her knees on the floor, with her hands still tied and the blindfold mask in place.

"Open your mouth," he ordered.

Isabelle complied without any resistance, opening her mouth wide to receive his long, thick penis that was already throbbing for more. Holding her head to control his movements going in and out, he made her suck and lick him to his satisfaction. When he couldn't hold the teasing anymore, he shot another load right down her throat, moaning while locking her head in place for her to swallow all of it.

"No inhibition. Or do you want to stop the *Last Tango*?" he panted.

"No inhibition," she whimpered, her heart beating furiously with the anticipation of what would come next from this absolutely unpredictable sexual encounter. She thought she couldn't take it any- more, but she would allow him to do whatever he wanted. Her dark- est fantasy had never even come close to what she was experiencing now. He lifted her from the floor and carried her gently back to bed. He opened her legs and inserted a finger in her ass and another in her vagina. He stroked her clit with his hot, wet tongue making her pussy once again drip in agony. Her body quivered in intense bliss. As he increased the movement of his fingers and tongue, he made her come again, feeling her powerful orgasm and delighting in the juice flowing down her thighs. She had never come twice in a row like that. She couldn't believe what he was capable of.

"Are you comfortable? Do you want anything?" he asked afterward.

"Yes—I want to feel you inside me. Now," she whispered, wriggling her body in expectation. "You make me so horny . . ."He let out a loud laugh. "Be patient, ma chèrie. I love working on your hot body. But let me work on the canvas for a bit while you rest and wait for my next turn. I'm not done fucking you."

He walked back to the canvas, leaving her in bed, still blindfolded and handcuffed—naked, exposed, and vulnerable. All she could hear was his heavy breathing and the soft sounds of brushstrokes on the canvas. Isabelle had no idea of the passing time when she sensed his presence next to her again. She felt his lips brushing against hers, and her skin tingled. His strong, square hands squeezed her tits and his fingers pinched her nipples, pulling them up and down, slapping and hardening them. She suddenly felt a painful pressure and realized he was attaching clamps on her erect nipples, exerting just enough force to make her moan in an agonizing sensation. The chain that joined the clamps fell on her chest, and she felt overpowered by the stranger's sexual desire once more. His hands trailed her tense body all the way down until he opened her legs to expose her again. He pinched her clit, sliding a finger inside her to find she was ready for him.

"You're so wet for me."

He penetrated her, shoving his hard penis into her with such a sudden force that it made her wriggle and groan in utter delight. Held captive by the seducing stranger, her body pulsated with lust. She felt his member sliding inside her, thrusting deeper and pushing harder, helped by her own inner muscles tightening their hold on him. She let out a loud moan as she wrapped her legs around his waist. Her hips and body moved to the rhythm of his thrusting urgency until he reached his climax again, taking his hard member out of her rapidly to release himself on her firm belly. While her body still shuddered from the wild pleasure, his mouth came down on hers and he tasted her with hunger, their tongues exploring each other in lusty yearning.

When he removed the blindfold from her, Isabelle blinked, adjusting her eyes to the dim light of the studio. He looked at her with his smoky, mesmerizing green eyes, unlocked the handcuffs, and carefully loosened the clamps attached to her nipples. She whimpered.

"Painful?"

She nodded, feeling her sore nipples throbbing from the pinch of the clamps so well attached by his expert hands. He licked her nipples gently with firm, wet strokes, sending shocks of desire through her once again. His fingers tickled the curves of her hips with an erotic touch while her hands, now freed from the hand-cuffs, clutched firmly at his disheveled hair. She moved closer to him, feeling his hard length pressed against her. His lips found hers again and his tongue invaded her mouth in a breathless, ardent kiss. She was still panting when he released her.

"I have to finish the painting now. You can stay as long as you want. Make yourself comfortable. The bed is yours tonight."

He cupped her face with his strong hands and planted a moist kiss on her swollen lips. As he moved back to the working easel, she admired his perfect naked body and sighed at the view. He was unbelievably hot, and he made her lust for him like she'd never lusted for anyone in her life. She had barely touched him, and she longed to stroke his body with her tongue and her hands. Her last night in Paris had been much better than she had ever anticipated, but she wanted more of him.

—◊◊◊—

Isabelle opened her eyes, looked around, but didn't see him. She realized, to her frustration, that she had dozed off in the stranger's comfortable bed and had no idea what time it was. She got up, gathered her clothes that had been scattered all over the floor, and got dressed quickly. When she picked up her purse and found her cell phone, she noticed it was 10 a.m. She needed to check out of her hotel by noon. She still had enough time to catch her flight. She walked around the loft, confirming he was definitely not there. The easel was empty, and the canvas was gone. In its place, she found a note.

"Hello, my horny and beautiful stranger,

I was able to complete the sexiest painting of *Last Tango in Paris* because of you. Thank you for an unforgettable night. By the way, I'll be in New York next month to paint a scene from *An Affair to Remember*. Would you be around to play my version of it?"

Isabelle's eyes widened and she blushed as warm, tingling moisture formed between her legs, thinking he would fuck her again. She couldn't believe *Last Tango in Paris* would end with *An Affair to Remember*!

She wrote her phone number and a message on the bottom of the note, pinned the piece of paper back on the easel, smiled naughtily, and left the loft.

"Call me. New York is my territory. *An Affair to Remember* is my turn—my version. No inhibition."

OBJECTIFICATION

X. K. Tangley

KATHY WAS STANDING in the dining room at the back of the town house and studying a large book of French country houses held open in her arms. The big mirror in front of her reflected herself and the bright blue, cloud-smeared summer afternoon outside the French doors behind her. Her posture was perfect and lovely, as always. She was wearing a mid-thigh-length, soft white jumper dress that left her arms bare and hugged her breasts and waist, flaring loose around her hips.

For the hell of it, I reached under the book and lifted her skirt, slid my fingers down inside the elastic of her panties, parted her soft pubic fur, and laid my middle finger along and just inside the warmth of her outer lips. She didn't change expression or speak or flinch; she just kept reading the section she was supposed to review for the newspaper. She didn't chide me, shift the book and pull my hand out, or look up. She just finished the paragraph. I began to feel really silly, really rude, and generally pretty stupid and unsure. Her vulva was getting hotter and moister as I left my finger there.

She started reading the next paragraph. "Do you want to fuck?" she asked, again without moving or looking up. I blushed. She probably couldn't have said anything that would make me feel more like a shit, highlight better the pointless immaturity of what I was doing, or make me feel more of an asshole.

I licked my lips. Her sex was definitely hotter, now, and wetter. She looked up and raised an eyebrow slightly.

"Ah. I— I'm sorry," I said.

She smiled now. "If you don't want to fuck, why are you fingering me?"

I felt about two years old.

Because you're here. You're beautiful, and I could get away with it, and it was an impulse to be wanton, crazy. Maybe some way it shows contempt, power, ownership. Maybe it's ennui, idleness, like feeling avocados in the grocery store when you don't want avocados. I swallowed.

We'd had a really great night, last night. I didn't know if I could even be up for sex. It must have been about ownership. "I, uh, I'm a shit, Kathy. It just came over me. It disrespects you: it's childish, rude, and obnoxious. Objectification of you. Ownership, dominance maybe. I don't know why I did it. I'm sorry."

She had closed the book, and now she set it down on the table to her left and reached for my waist, starting to unfasten my pants. She cocked her head and smiled more. I felt wetness on my finger, the finger I still had inside her panties.

"That's very good feminist dialectic, Phil. You're well trained." She got my pants undone and then slid them down my hips. She took a little sidestep, her intimate flesh embracing my fingers tighter. "Objectification. Do you really think of me as an *object* when you have your hand in my pussy?"

I swallowed again. "No. I . . ." my heart was hammering. Her sex was really hot now. I swallowed. "You're a woman. You're—"

"I'm your woman, right?" She had her hands inside my underwear, stroking my cock and squeezing my balls. "That's why you said ownership: dominance, right? You know you can feel me up any time and I can't complain."

I didn't know that, really. I'd half expected she would slap me. Mostly, I expected some sort of outburst, and a silly argument about prudishness, and some sort of sorry childishness after my compulsive violation of her. I was getting harder the more she played with me.

She tossed back her long silky hair, smiled again, and changed the way she was stroking my dick, as if she knew what it wanted.

"Maybe you just thought it would be fun to play with my pussy. I love playing with your cock and balls. I can understand that."

She was squeezing and loosening the muscles of her vulva now and was quite wet. I stroked her clit with one finger, with my middle finger beginning to slip into her vagina. She pushed against it gently, tilting her pelvis with little thrusts.

I groaned. "Oh . . . God, yes. I love to play with your pussy. With all of you. With your tits. Your ass. I'm—"

"A man. Thank God." She was breathing quicker now, pulling my underwear down further, stroking and bouncing my rock-hard cock just the way I'd do it. She started pulling it down to the wood floor, urging me to kneel. I did. She pulled her panties down with her left hand, and I slipped my fingers into her up to the hilt, except thumb and forefinger, massaging her clitoris. She lifted my shirttails up with her left hand, pushing back on my belly. I sat on the floor. She moved over me and pushed my chest back.

"Lie down on your back, Phil. You never answered if you want to fuck." She grinned, pulled my hand out gently and took my cock into her, sucking it in, the muscular walls of her heat pulling it. I gasped. She began making a little circle on me, grinding her pubic bone against mine. "Too late now. Thrust, Phil. I'm using you."

I thrusted while she made her circle. I fingered her anus and rubbed her slippery clit the way she liked. She whimpered. Pretty soon she was shuddering and arching her back, and there was juice soaking my belly and wicking into her skirt, making the white fabric translucent.

Her nipples were poking hard against her bodice. She panted and looked at me. Then she unzipped her dress down her back and tossed it over a chair. She unhooked her bra and threw it aside. She leaned forward and undid my shirt buttons, panting, her breasts swinging.

She rolled my nipples in her fingers and then sat back and started rocking on me, moaning. We were back in the rhythm, without the extra clothes. She leaned forward over me. I sucked one nipple into my mouth, and she smiled wider.

It was hypnotic. Her riding me and coming, me thrusting into her, slack-jawed, marveling. She was so lovely, so hot, and her pleasure was so open, so satisfying. I felt like I could go forever enjoying it, not coming.

After forty minutes to an hour, she took a deep breath, leaned forward on me, kneading the muscles of my neck—trapezius, somebody called them—panting and looking concerned. "Hey. Can't you come?"

My dick was sort of doing Zen, by now, imitating a wood block—just *being*. It was kind of beyond sex, beyond desire. Conquered desire and hard as wood. A fucking mudra, so to speak. Buddhist, tantric, zoned to the gills. I was gasping, covered in sweat, flying in the groove. "Yeah. I can probably come, if I turn my dick back on. Right now it's just locked into being a fuck stick for you."

She blinked. "You don't *want* to come?"

"Kathy, sure I want to come." *Sometime.* "But if I come, I get a minute of release. If I soak in you fucking me, I get hours of ecstasy." *I'm inside you, tasting you, feeling you, smelling you, heated by you, fondling you, cradled by you, locked into you.* "Inside. You."

She blinked again and closed her mouth. She blushed. She reached around with her left hand and felt my swollen balls, the engorged base of my member.

"Phil, that's so—spiritual?" She paused. "Perversely using? Altruistic?" She laughed. "Psychotic? Sweet?" She squeezed my balls again, and I groaned. "They say on those TV ads not to stay hard too long, or it may ruin your dick. I don't want to ruin your dick. Or make your balls explode."

I tried to get her moving again. "Four hours. We've got hours to go."

She rocked on me, a different rhythm, not panting, her eyes on me, not lost in lust. "Four hours of being hard; not four hours of fucking. And then you're supposed to be in the ER. I want you to come. How do we turn your dick back on?" Kathy asked.

She stopped moving and just sat on me, squatted, legs open, supporting herself on her knees and calves.

I pulled her dress off the chair and spread it on the floor next to me. "Doggy, kneel on that and let me get you from behind. Then roll over and I'll fill you with cum."

She climbed off me, knelt on all fours, and looked over her shoulder, reaching around to squeeze me as I pushed into her. "Promise? That you'll fill me with cum when I can see your face?"

"Yes," I grunted. She made her circle while I thrusted and panted, my neck swelling and face turning bright red. Her left hand, under us, rubbed my balls.

I grabbed her and flipped her over, holding her back off the floor. I laid her down, knees out and up, and rammed into her as hard as I could, exploding while she pulled my hips into her. I poured sweat and cried out, pumping fire out of my burning cock. I shivered like a dog shitting peach pits. I heard her chuckle and felt her hands on me, all over me—gentle, like magic, releasing my tension.

When I could see her again, her eyes were happy and she was smiling like a Madonna. She did a sit-up, hips pinned by mine, my dick inside her, and kissed me. She held herself up with one arm and ran the other fingers through my hair. Then she kissed me again.

"I see why you liked watching me come," she said. "It was wonderful to see you so totally mind blown."

I was grinning as wide as the Joker. "Yeah." I felt like nirvana. "Maybe blowing my—"

She reached around behind and under me and rubbed them. She laughed. "They're looser, now. They don't feel like they're strangled anymore."

I was still gasping some. "No. They're less tight now."

She laid back and I followed her, rubbing my face in her breasts, kissing her throat, and kissing her lips. She stroked my head, smoothing my hair back.

After a few minutes, she asked when I was going to pull out of her. "Cream pie, right?" she asked. "That's what they call it online. You want to see the cream pie you made?"

I shook my head. "Yes. They do."

"Let's see."

I leaned back and pulled out of her. The magical white purity of the Manicheans followed, rich and thick, out of her still-dilated body. She giggled. "I feel it! It feels like you did fill me."

She touched herself with a finger and brought it up, dripping white. She sighed and looked at me. "That was fun, right? More fun than getting your dick deflated in the ER."

I was still shaking my head. "Yeah. More fun than the ER." I moved up between her open legs and smoothed her hair back off her sweaty face. "More intense than watching you. But I love watching you."

She pulled me down on her, and I felt my cum dripping out of her, down my balls, onto her dress. "You can do both."

She kissed my eyes. "And you can put your hand in my panties whenever you want." She laughed. "As long as I can use you afterward . . . and you can use me." Her eyes sparkled. "But we aren't *objects*."

"No; we're lovers," I said.

"People."

"Man and goddess."

"Woman and hopeless romantic."

She let go of me and sat up as I moved back to give her space. She pulled her dress between her legs and stood, wrapping it around her loins to contain the drips. She held it with one hand, reached for me with the other, and headed for the stairs. "Let's take a shower. Then I have to finish my review, and you have to start writing your story."

She squeezed my hand. "I'm glad this dress is washable."

RE-ROUTING

Copper Hayes

I TAKE THE KIDS to school every day at the same time: 7:40. On the dot. We always take a different route. At first I used it as a teaching tool, finding new items for an alphabet game or counting the number of oak trees we passed.

Now, slumped in the back seat, they bury their heads, clicking on their devices. They're not watching or wanting to learn much of anything from me. I find it ridiculous that a ten- and a twelve-year-old can't ride a school bus, but I'm the only mom in our "circle" with that unpopular mindset, so I cart their little asses around day in and day out.

I still take a different route each morning. It's a small indulgent concession to the rut of a life I'm leading.

There's a new house going up. The construction foreman catches my eye and my imagination. He looks like the men I used to favor. Longish hair pulled back in a ponytail. Bulges that aren't a beer belly. My eyes follow him. I almost miss the stop sign, slamming the brake pedal with a little squeal. He looks up but looks right past me in this godawful square, silver SUV.

My mouth goes dry, and my eyes dart to the rearview mirror: loose, mousy brown strings of hair escape from a rag-tag ponytail, looking like litter along my cheekbones. Some women can pull off the messy-ponytail look—the kind they spend twenty minutes arranging. I check the mirror again. Not happening here. My hair looks like a do you'd find on a decades-old rag doll that had been given to the dog six years ago.

I pull into the line to let the kids out. It will creep forward at a pace designed to piss me off. Little shits finishing a text before they can be bothered to exit their mom-driven limos. If I'd known I was going to spend most of my time chauffeuring two perfectly healthy, hearty children around, I would have stuck to raising beagles. I dash the traitorous non-maternal thought.

Think about Stan instead. He looks like a Stan. Tanned. Taut. Trouble. I pick at my cuticles, needing something to do with my hands that won't get me arrested for lewd public behavior.

"Bye, Mom." Josh bolts out the back door, one shoe untied, the lace threatening to send him to the nurse's office with skinned palms and a bleeding knee.

"Don't forget to pick me up early. I have ballet." Jordan slides out of the car without a backward glance and certainly no sign of a thank-you.

I'll bet his eyes are grey. A blue bordering on a storm-cloud gray. And his hands: just enough callous to grit against the skin. I swallow and creep forward to the line's exit. And freedom: at least for seven blissful hours.

I retrace my route, slowing as my pumpkin of a chariot eases past the construction site. He's got a set of plans in his hand, gesturing to a bank of windows. The men around him nod. I would too. I would nod, comply, and obey.

I screech into my driveway, pull out my cell, and make an appointment to get my hair cut and colored. I call back. They can fit me in to wax a few things while I'm processing. Multi-tasking was always my strong suit. Wonder how I'll do with multi-men.

My nipples want to find out. They feel like balloons filled with warm honey, the viscous pressure congesting the feeling. My left fingers reach across to my right breast and toy with the sensitive point through the light padding of my big, wide, harness of a bra.

Lingerie store. I add it to my checklist. Contemplating a seduction is way more fun than planning menus.

Trimmed, shaped, colored, and waxed, I look good. I even make this tank of a vehicle look good. OK, that's a stretch, but it's gotta look more interesting.

I test my theory and coast by Stan's current place of employment. Twice. I see him on the second lap around the block. He's hauling a stack of two-by-fours across his left shoulder. I lift my foot off the gas pedal and eat him with my eyes. A horn jolts me out of a fantasy that found me kneeling, looking up, and stroking a cock as long and wide as one of those boards. I managed to choke it down my throat and still look beautiful. His hands were on either side of my face, and his knees were starting to buckle.

He looks up when the horn sounds. He smiles and lifts his right hand in a quick salute. Then he continues into the framed-up house with his load. The impatient driver behind me honks again. I speed up, trying to go as fast as my pounding heart.

I'm quiet that night at dinner. No one notices my hair, and I won't let anyone notice my wax job. Being invisible gives me a headache. I soak in a hot bath and play mind tapes. He's in a hard hat and wearing a tool belt, jackhammering his most efficient and effective tool into me as I bend over a sawhorse. My fingers are inadequate, but they find me slick and warm. I sink two of them to the hilt, then move them in a slow, widening circle, opening up my cunt for that concrete, colossal cock. I shudder, and the oily essence of me floods my palm.

It's the best orgasm I've had in months, but it's not enough.

Tuesday morning, 7:40 on the dot, I wind my way through the same maze of streets. The little heathens belted into the backseat won't notice. They didn't say a word about my makeup and the tight top I'm wearing. Recognition creases Stan's face into a grin. I glance in the rearview mirror as I gas it through the intersection. He must see the want in me.

I get nails and toes done on Wednesday. Red. Daring. Sparkly with just a touch of glitter. They'll stand out against his tanned face when he licks and teases each piggy with a slow, taunting tongue tango. His pink tongue will circle, dart, and inch up my shivering, pulsing leg.

"Think you need another coat?" The manicurist looks up and frowns. "You OK? You look a little flushed."

I squeeze my thighs, smothering the fire in between them, and check the coverage on the polish. "It's a little warm in here." I fan myself with a magazine folded open to a story on achieving better orgasms. "Yes, one more coat. A light one."

She bends to her task, and I return to Stan. In my mind, he presses those calloused palms into the very inner tops of my thighs and splays his fingers. My cunt quakes. He murmurs some terrible little warning about making me wait, making it last, making it desperate.

I want to push; I want him to push. Instead, he blows a warm, small puff of air against the lips covering his final destination. Just enough to quiver my gut.

"Please," I implore.

"Not yet," he replies.

"OK. All done," the manicurist says. She mists my nails with a fast-drying miracle spray and hurries me out of her chair, making room for her next client. The seat is damp.

I need a vibrator. I drive to the sex shop that occupies expensive real estate on a main street far enough from my neighborhood that I don't have to wear a disguise. The wall of fake-y shaky dicks overwhelms me. A young man with tattoos, inch-wide discs piercing his ears, and a Mohawk is surprisingly professional and well-versed. I leave the shop with a fleshy, realistic rubber dick about eight inches long and an inch and a half wide. It's smaller than Stan's, but it will be a good training toy.

The sex shop salesman also seduced me into parting with one hundred and fifty dollars plus tax for a magic wand. I can say it's a shoulder massager, but I'll have to keep my pussy smell cleaned off its big, bulbous head.

The house is quiet when I get home. A rush of gratitude, then grating need, sweeps through me as I walk from room to room, making sure I'm alone.

I yank off my pants, spread a towel on the end of the bed, plug in my mechanical massager, and nestle the rubber cock by my side. I depress the switch, and the vibration rips up my arm. My toes curl. I butterfly my legs wide and hover the whirring wand over my clit. I take a deep breath and allow it to rest against salty, slippery skin.

I'm shocked when my back arches into an impossible backbend, and a shuddering orgasm makes me fling the wand across the room and clamp my thighs together to hold on to the waves of surging ooze and tingle. I flop back, and everything from my waist down feels like it's gyrating to throbbing, tribal rhythms. My throat aches as if I've been screaming at a peewee football game.

When I can breathe, I push up and look for my new favorite thing in the entire universe. It took a small divot out of the paint where it hit the wall. I roll off the bed and crawl across the room to make sure the wand hadn't suffered any damage when I let it fly. I may have to harness it to my body to keep from denting the wall. It purrs into life and I decide to post an anonymous testimonial on the company's website. This baby is worth every penny.

Reluctantly I unplug it, knowing if it touched me again I would never stop. I hide my new BFF in a drawer filled with sexy nightgowns, dusty with disuse.

Thursday morning, Josh pipes up from the back seat. "Hey, Mom. We went this way yesterday."

A little guilt and a wad of amazement clogs my throat.

Stan and I make eye contact as I drive past. I can't find my voice to answer my ten-year-old, but he's already killing zombies on his phone. My eyes glue to the rearview mirror. Stan's gaze follows me. How will I make it through the weekend?

My new demi bra's lace rasps against my nipples, which threaten to escape the plunging confines. I tug down my low neckline and free my left nipple with an elongating twist. Cool air licks at the escapee.

I leave it out even after I pull into the drop-off line in front of the school. Jordan's homeroom teacher just misses the daring display. I shrug it back under-cover as she leans in my passenger window.

"Did Jordan give you my note about helping with the end-of-year party?" she asks.

Jordan thrusts an envelope over the front seat back and then slides out of the SUV and skips across the courtyard. She disappears into the redbrick school building.

Her teacher and I exchange knowing smirks. She glances at my chest before she pushes away from the car. Unseemly bulges tent my knit top like tiny flashlights. I find an odd empathy for men with elicit protuberances telling all their secrets.

I remember the impressive selection of nipple clips at the sex store. I also have clothespins at home. I decide to take the frugal, efficient route. I have work to do today and can't spare the time for another sex-shop trip. Although, I hope they have a frequent-shopper punch-card program. I'm going to have to clean out that locking trunk in the back of my closet to store all my new purchases.

I prowl the neighborhood, lapping the new subdivision as I watch the crew's activity. Just like yesterday, everyone leaves at 11:30. Everyone except Stan. He trails them at 11:45, hefting his muscled limbs into the cab of a Ram pickup truck.

I'd like him to ram into me.

My hand wanders to the space between my legs, and I press fingers against my jeans. I'm going to have a wreck.

On Friday morning I change my route slightly. I pass Stan going the opposite direction. His head cocks to the side as he lets his eyes crawl down my neck.

The drop-off line crawls, halts, starts, stops, and jerks. Finally, Jordan and Josh launch themselves into their day, giving me leave to really start mine.

I get a ticket speeding to the car-rental agency. The paperwork is more daunting than the clipboard filled with forms my gynecologist hands me at each annual visit. I scribble details in the blanks, check boxes, and sign and date at the bottom. Finally, the fluffy, fat young woman behind the desk drops a set of keys into my palm. The cold metal warms as I curl my fingers into a fist.

The convertible Corvette is Mickey-Mouse-pants red and costs me most of the hoarded cash in my secret stash. An expensive but delicious joyride.

I have time for a Starbucks run. I take the long way there, watching heads turn to see who's driving this hot roar of a sports car. I may need to save up for one of these. I should be able to afford one about the time the kids graduate.

I sit at an outside table close to my red chariot. A black thong cleaves the crack of my ass under leggings tucked into knee-high, high-heeled red boots. My boat-neck tunic covers a matching bra, but the cling of it doesn't hide my curves. No sugar or carbs for four days flattened my tiny belly paunch.

I check my watch and walk my empty cup to a trashcan, inviting eyes with my saunter. I take my time unlocking the door, posing beside my red man magnet. One man swallows, his Adam's apple broadcasting his want. Another arches an eyebrow. A young man purses his lips, his gaze leaving the car to linger on my ass. I bask in the appraisal.

When I roar out of the parking lot, I lift my hand to my audience in a little wave. At exactly 11:43, I coast to a stop in front of the construction site. I let the car idle, my heart running hard in my chest. An imaginary poultice blankets my body, bringing every nerve ending to a head.

Stan walks out of the Tyvek-covered project, head down. I gun the engine, dragging his glance my way. It morphs into a stare and then into a lopsided grin that makes his eyes tell stories.

"New ride?" he asks. His voice is molten chocolate lava cake with a scoop of vanilla-bean ice cream on the side.

I just smile and drink him in.

"Can I help you?" He draws closer to me, his crotch at eye level. His dick stirs.

I test the bulk of it in my left hand. "I think you can."

He grows against my palm. It's not quite as big as I imagined but is a more-than-serviceable size. "Want to see the house?" he asks.

"Splendid idea," I reply. I switch off the throb of the engine. He opens my door and offers me his calloused hand. His finger curls into my palm. Saliva floods my tongue.

I unfold from the low-lying machine, tremors threatening to bring me to my knees right there on the sidewalk. I walk beside him with precise steps, my heels clicking on the newly poured cement. I hope those sounds drown out the thudding in my chest.

We don't make it more than three feet inside the front door. We turn into each other, and his tongue roams my mouth while his hands find the hem of my tunic and lift it, without asking permission, up and over my head. He steps back an arm's length and traces his gaze in a slow circuit over my exposed skin.

I want to hurl myself at him, but he shakes his head. "Let me look. Just a minute more."

Every instinct tells me to fold my arms into a shield, but I clamp them to my side and withstand his scrutiny. He puts his hands on my shoulders and rotates me around. His fingers scamper over the small of my back. Sensations blaze from my core, infiltrating every crevasse and curve. His fingers mark a deft path up the knobbiness of my backbone, lingering on each bump with a searing caress.

Without fumbling, he unhooks my bra, using both hands to brush the pieces aside. I shudder. His hands, big and painfully light, flutter me into a spasm. One finger from each hand nudges my bra straps over the cliffs of my shoulders. They hang momentarily, then tumble down my arms. My black lace bra falls and mingles with sawdust.

His breath bristles the tiny hairs on the back of my neck. I drop my head. He flicks my offering with his tongue. I am a living, breathing, pulsing sensation.

He circles me then in a slow, appraising dance. I decide to lead.

My hands skim my sides and come up under my breasts, offering their heft to him. His eyes fuse to my nipples. He swallows.

I move up to him, just short. My fingers work the buttons on his work shirt. It's soft from repeated washings yet stiff with this morning's sweat. He smells like Zest soap and clean dust. I tiptoe up to peel his shirt off his shoulders and halfway down his arms. I leave it tangling his hands into a bind.

It's my turn to circle and assess. I find tiny blemishes on his perfection: a half-moon scar, a mole darkened by the sun, deodorant caked in the tufts of hair under his arms. I drop to a squat so I can nose his belly button. He sucks in his six-pack and I play his ribs like a xylophone.

I want to hurry. I want to wait. I mostly just want.

I shimmy up, my tongue leaving a slug trail as I straighten my trembling legs. I press my breasts into his chest. He shudders a held-breath loose. His chest hairs tickle. I grind my nipples against the rough of his skin.

He struggles his arms out of the twisted sleeves in a slow-motion fury. His hands find my ass and cup the cheeks, pulling me up against a rigid bulge behind the zipper of his jeans. With infuriating deliberation, he flexes his fingers away and then digs them back into my flesh, kneading my ass like a heart surgeon would massage a failed organ. Throbs beat in time with his delicious torment. He growls. His fingers delve into the crack of my ass, and he pulls my cheeks apart. My pussy gapes.

He backs me up until I'm pinned against a workbench. His fingers inch up and curl into the waistband of my leggings. He rolls them down in a perfect slow waltz, uncovering my cunt. He stops and leans toward me till I arch over the rough edge of the table. His mouth finds mine, his lips barely parted, and tenderizes me. We explore-kiss for long seconds that turn into a minute. His tongue tip teases, but he doesn't venture in.

I am wired, weak, willing.

An electric charge starts where he plugs the tip of his middle finger into the uppermost cleft of my cunt. It swirls around my clit, the nub of it swelling into a tiny, needy cock. He brings his thumb into play, pinching and rolling my clit-cock. He's maddening me. I come and I cry. He licks my tears as he works his fingers deeper into my folds, finding places that need finding. Fondling.

Finally, he slides his middle finger into my vagina with a prolonged plunge. I clench my cunt, locking the fleshy channel around his finger, refusing to let it leave. He curls his middle digit, and I bolt straight up. So that's my G spot. I cover his hand with mine, finding a slim wedge of space, and worm my finger next to his. He presses it into the thorny terrain on the roof of my vaginal canal. We probe and flex together till I quake, and a viscous spray covers our hands. He withdraws, leaving my finger buried in my own cunt. His slippery hands massage my cum into my breasts.

I brush my G spot, greedy for another orgasm. It wrenches through me.

"My turn." He picks me up off the workbench, sets my high-heeled boots on the floor, spins me around, and bends me over the table. My smeared breasts pick up flecks of sawdust and grit. I push my ass into his crotch and find his hand fumbling with his zipper. He presses me down against the table and shucks his pants down past his knees. My leggings pin my legs together, but he burrows his cock between my legs and thrusts with precision into his target.

He fucks like a mad man: slow, driving into me an inch at a time. Maddening.

I screw myself onto his cock, wanting him to punish me, to pound me into senselessness. But he's determined. And controlled. And deliberate. When his pelvic bone mates with mine, he is home. And I'm glad for his stillness. My cunt swaddles his cock.

He starts to pulse slow throbs, plunging the fullness of himself farther, deeper. His fingers dig into my hips, and a gurgle wrests from his throat.

Now it's his turn. He anchors my ass with his hands and pistons and pumps. He moves in and out of me with a relentless rhythm that starts an avalanche. I overflow, my body emptying into my cunt, fertilizing my swollen lips, harvesting my clit.

A hum reverberates from his gut and with three savage, lovely thrusts, he spills and folds over me. We lay that way until my hands and arms start to prick and tingle, needing blood flow.

There's a noise outside. The crew.

He eases back, and I frantically search for my long-lost tunic top. He grins in a lopsided, sated way that curls the left side of his mouth into an invitation. He reads my frantic mind. "No—I gave them the afternoon off."

I stop scrambling for cover.

He puts his calloused, lovely hands under my armpits and lifts me back up on the workbench as if I am a waif. He takes the heel of my left boot in his right hand and uses his left to help leverage it off. He sets it down and then relieves me of the right boot.

"I love these boots," he says. "Sexy."

He strips off my leggings and my thong like a magician pulling a cloth out from under a fully set table.

"I didn't have lunch." He eases my knees apart and up. "Mind if I eat you?"

I don't mind.

❧ COMPLICATED ☙

C.S. Julia

BERNADINE WASN'T RUNNING from her problems; it was more of a calculated retreat.

Three days ago, she had walked out of her home without a word. It was a long time since she had been completely alone. No one called her. No one texted. No one did anything.

The sun crawled up the sky over the Gulf of Mexico. In the distance, light danced on the water while waves crashed against the brown sand just beyond her deck. Majestic whitecaps hit the beach, taking tolls and claiming the land like Spanish Conquistadors. From her deck, Bernadine searched for people, but there were none.

Bernadine was at Pink Sky, the family beach house. Time there was supposed to be happy, but, as usual, she was alone. Her mother had taken the kids on a vacation to Italy. Bernadine wasn't invited. The three weeks of Christmas vacation were booked solid for her children. Her mom's sense of impending mortality resulted in her desire to spend every possible moment with her only grandchildren: Mary, 16; Martha, 17; and Laz, short for Lazarus, 19.

At 18, Bernadine had been spunky, ready for life, newly married to a respectable man, and pregnant. Today at 38, Bernadine was exhausted, contemplating separation, and in no danger of becoming pregnant—by anyone. Sex was normally a requirement for such things.

The fresh breeze off the Gulf of Mexico blew her long, black hair off her face. It may have been late December, but the temperature was only 54 degrees. That's Texas. The mid-weight cashmere sweater over a long-sleeved t-shirt and a pair of yoga pants was enough to stave off the chill in the air.

Bernie was a curvy girl who had become a curvy woman. No amount of Zumba, Tae Bo, or yoga ever sculpted her down to anything less. She was healthy, and that was enough. However, Bernie was oblivious to the way she turned heads when she entered a space. With even more than a stunning tan complexion, an hourglass figure, and a bright smile, her very presence could warm a room.

Almost twenty years of marriage brought her to this exact moment. The probability that her husband was working today was minimal, at best. Once he knew that Bernie's mother was taking the kids, he claimed a need to work. He would make the most of his time and "finish some 'end-of-the-year' things."

Bernie's hopes were open wounds in which he had poured salt. She knew there had been someone else for a while, but her faith in the ability to get past it was strong. After all, she had been through so much in the years since they met. She had lost a child, buried two parents, and survived his one-night stand with his ex-wife, unknowingly and knowingly shared him with other women, and navigated parenting.

Life was exhausting, and Bernie was done. She just didn't feel like there was any fight left in her. Giving 100% for almost twenty years had taken a large toll on her.

When Bernie realized that she wasn't broken-hearted over the thought, something shifted, a weight lifted, and her mind spun. She had expected it to hurt more, to sting more. It didn't. This was the real reason she sat at the beach house contemplating her purpose, her place, and her marital status.

Does Julian love this woman? Do I love Julian?

—◊◊◊—

Bernie pulled the coffee mug to her face and, upon realizing it had gone cold, flung it violently at the railing of the deck, relishing the sound and effect of visual brokenness. A damn cup was more company than her husband was. She stomped past the double French doors, walked into the first-floor master bedroom, stripped off her layers, and replaced them with running shorts and a t-shirt. Without locking the door, she ran out of the house as if it was about to receive a direct hit from a hurricane. When her running shoes worked, her mind rested.

—◊◊◊—

"Ma'am. Ma'am. Are you OK?"

"Yes. Yes. I was just tired." Bernie turned over and opened her eyes. She squinted against the bright sun. It sat higher in the sky, burning a halo against the man's figure. A hand reached out to her. She took it.

"I thought you were dead. You looked washed up," the man said as he helped Bernie off the wet sand.

She yanked her hand away. "Thanks. You should have left me, then. Or do you frequently collect washed-up old ladies?"

"That's *not* what I meant. But it sounds like someone has issues," he said and then laughed lightly. His eyes were a soft brown, as was his hair. The cut wasn't exactly short, but it was not long, either, and it sported a soft wave.

Bernie stopped dead in her tracks as the warmth of his laughter echoed through her. She laughed in return. "I guess I just sounded washed up and bitter. Sorry about that."

"Not a problem, ma'am."

"Bernadine." Introductions seemed like a good idea.

"Gibson," he replied.

"Really? Like the guitar?"

"Exactly. My parents were in a garage band together."

"Of course, and you are their love child," she said.

"Sounds strange to you, a woman I found sleeping on the beach?" Though they hadn't consciously realized it, they were walking.

"True enough. Score one, guitar boy."

—⁓—

Bernie stopped and sat on the sand. Gibson stopped with her. He was amused by her wit and taken in by her easiness. She removed her tennis shoes and socks. Gibson inspected her tanned legs and smiled as he saw her toes, perfect French nails, just like her hands. He always found that kind of attention to detail belonged to women who were out of his league but too hot to resist.

Gibson had taken the time to appreciate her body as she lay on the beach, face resting on her arms and pert ass in the air. He'd swallowed hard when the wind blew her running shorts up enough to reveal a sweet, tanned bottom. His midsection had applauded as he inspected the tattoo peeking from low on her back, an array of swirls and colors. Gibson could tell she was breathing, so there was no need to rush his assessment of her small waist and rounded bottom. The curve of her neck aligned with her shiny black hair.

But right now, her toenails sparkled in the sun while her body reacted to the slight chill in the air. Hearing her gentle, sex-flavored laughter told him everything he needed to know about Bernadine. This was not a girl; this was a woman. Gibson could see that her shoes were soaked. She had likely been running close to the water's edge.

"You're out pretty far . . . no houses or cars for at least a mile. Thought maybe you were hurt. But you look good," Gibson said.

"I went out for my run and lost track of how far I'd gone. I can make it back home, though. Slower without shoes."

"Home?" He checked her hand for a ring. No ring—just a tan line on the most complicated finger.

"Yes. Thank you for waking me up. A sunburn isn't something I wanted for Christmas."

Gibson watched as she stood. His eyes could not help gravitating toward her breasts. They were nice and sized perfectly for his large hands, with some to spare. He was so focused on her hard tips that he barely heard when she cleared her throat.

After getting his attention refocused, she said, "Sorry, the beach was empty and I didn't think I would need a sweater. I hate to be a distraction. You were probably running. Don't let me hold you up." Her poor choice of words brought a smile to both of them. Bernie's cheeks bloomed into pink perfection.

"I was done. I'm parked close by. It'll cause me actual physical pain, but I'll loan you a sweater so you can cover up."

"Physical pain, huh?" she laughed. It had been a while since someone had flirted with her like this.

"Too much? I've never been good at this. But I'm sure you've heard every line possible."

"Not really. When I was younger, maybe. But the lines have changed for us old, washed-up ladies."

"That's not fair. And Bernie, my car is up ahead. Do you want that sweater?" he asked.

"I'm a little sandy and wouldn't want to ruin it. Besides, how would you get it back?"

"That's easy. I was going to walk you to your house while trying to get your number."

"Really? Wow. Thanks, but I'm married. And, you look my son's age," she stated.

Gibson put a hand on his heart as if there was actual physical pain. He wanted her so bad that he could almost taste her lips. "First of all, your husband is a damn lucky man. And secondly, there's no way you have a kid who's almost thirty."

"Ha!" she laughed. "Only a man would round his age up! No, my son is younger. It doesn't matter anyway because you called me washed-up earlier," she said, chuckling lightly.

"Wait for me and I'll get you that sweater," Gibson said while walking toward a beige Jeep parked close to the dunes. He loved feisty women, and this woman was making it so it didn't matter if there was a husband. Gibson wanted to get to know Bernadine a little bit more.

Returning with a sweater, a smile, and a goal, he placed a hooded jacket over her shoulders. "It'll remind your husband how lucky he is."

Bernie looked away. The statement went down like spoiled milk and she spilled the words without thinking. "He has someone better to do. He won't ever see this."

There was a thick silence for a bit, and then Gibson was back to smiling. "So, not only can I walk you home, but I can also have a glass of water while you get ready for our lunch date."

At this, Bernie looked at him with tear-swollen eyes. "What is wrong with you? I already told you, I'm married."

Gibson replied, "Honestly, I don't know. I'm normally smarter than this. Married women are trouble. But you . . . you're so fucking beautiful and funny, and from the moment I saw you on the beach. . . . Well, I'm not giving up now. Your husband may very well be the stupidest man alive if he leaves a window cracked for some sneaky bastard to join his wife in bed." He put his hand around her shoulders.

Bernie threw her head back and laughed. "You are so good for my ego."

"So, that's a yes."

"Coffee?" Bernie asked.

"It's not morning, anymore," Gibson replied.

"Then . . ."

"Just sex?" he asked coyly.

"No."

"A drink? At the Snapper Grill?" Gibson asked, making every effort to open the window of opportunity.

"My house. Just chatting on the deck, being neighborly. That's all."

"I can work with that. Um, so just to be sure, no crazy husband marching in with a shotgun, right? I'm perfectly willing to die for the right lady, but if we're just neighborly, hmmm."

"We can forgo the drinks and neighborly talk—" Bernie started.

"And go straight into the sex part? I'd love that." Gibson interrupted.

"No. We could just be nothing like we were before you called me washed up."

"Well, that is completely unacceptable."

—◦⁄⁄◦—

Three hours later, Bernie was on her fourth gin and Diet Coke and Gibson was on his third iced whiskey. The conversation was easy after the initial breakdown of her marital situation. Bernie told Gibson that Julian, her husband, was either spending Christmas with his lover or was "working," and she was sure it was the former. So, she was on what should have been a Hail Mary pass for their marriage. When Julian refused to come to the beach house, Bernie threatened to leave him. Julian's response was obviously not a sign of a man fighting for a marriage he wanted.

That was Bernie's stopping point. She refused to mention the man after that. Gibson couldn't see past how relaxed she had become after getting out of that conversation, so he didn't push. Gibson and Bernie talked about their childhoods, how they both loved the ocean, and everything else. To the outside eye, they looked like the dearest of friends.

In Gibson's mind, nothing seemed simpler. He liked her. He'd never met a woman like her: so easy and yet a little intimidating. She was a refined, intricate puzzle that he could see spending much time solving. His sweater came off her once she was inside serving the drinks.   They were on their first drink when he asked about food to even out the effect of the alcohol on empty stomachs. He'd been asking to take her out again, but she brought out the only thing she could find: olives, cheese, and grapes. It was obvious to Gibson that Bernadine's idea of grocery shopping for the beach was dictated by anger: coffee and alcohol, mostly.

The laughter went through Gibson as Bernie narrated the adventure of parenting. He followed her as she padded around gracefully in her small running shorts and perfectly tight t-shirt. Her curves were a song begging to be played. When she bent over as she looked into the mostly empty fridge, he could hardly keep from launching forward and taking her there. Every male instinct in his hard body desired to claim this woman. Now he knew more about her situation and didn't give a rat's ass about complicating the situation further. Any man stupid enough to let this woman out of his sight, much less cheat on her, had this coming. Gibson knew he would pursue Bernie until she was his. For him, that was the only acceptable outcome.

———

"Bernie, you're drunk and I'm getting there. Either let me feed you or take you, because I'm getting to the point where I don't care about dealing with a jealous husband."

She was sitting across from him at the kitchen table, watching him move, flex, harden. Her mind wandered too far south. She'd hungered for months, and every move he made opened her appetite.

In the least convincing voice ever, Bernie said, "You have to leave now. I'm sorry."

"But we've only been talking, I haven't tried anything, and you sound like you need a friend. We could have a friendly lunch and sober up."

"Gibson," she said, almost breathless, and shook her head no. Bernie got up and started walking toward the door.

Like his life depended on it, Gibson followed, catching up to her quickly. As he was about to reach for her arm and beg reprieve, she turned right into him.

Her breasts pressed up against his chest. Quickly, Gibson wrapped his arm around her waist and leaned into her ear, "I want you."

In a raw physical reaction to his voice and hands, Bernie ran her hands up his firm chest. She swallowed. The contours of his body, the sweet scent of man, and the husk in his voice were more than she could handle on a sober day. Today it was impossible. She found herself melting into him. Having needed comfort for so long, Bernie could not pull herself away.

His hands moved at a snail's pace down into her shorts, along the curve of her bottom. A warm fire was left in the path. She felt him hardening against her, a statement of intent. Suddenly, in contrast to his slow and patient behavior, he pushed her against the wall of the living area and his mouth came down hungrily on hers.

"God, Bernie. You taste good."

"I'm not thinking straight, Gib."

"Let me make love to you," Gibson said in between ravishing her mouth and her breasts through her shirt. He leaned back, grabbed the hem of her tee, and pulled it over her head, exposing her overflowing sports bra.

Her head spun as he bit through the thin cotton. A deep guttural moan escaped her. She arched herself into his mouth while pulling at his shirt in a desperate need to feel his skin against hers.

"I'll take that as a yes," Gibson mumbled through a mouthful of tender breasts.

Before he finished saying it, her legs wrapped around his waist and he carried her to the sofa. There he sat, with her astride and enjoyed the deep grinding she offered in response to his kisses. He pulled her sports bra over her head. Then he feasted upon her. His roughened fingers delved deep inside her soft, wet core. From there it was a feeding frenzy for the sex-starved.

With complete and utter disregard for her comfort, and much to her pleasure, Gibson bucked Bernie off his lap, throwing her into a sitting position on the sofa, next to him. Getting in front of her, he yanked off her shorts and underwear. Gibson pushed her legs apart roughly.

"Damn, but you are beautiful," he said as he dropped to his knees before a naked Bernie and moved his hungry mouth to the spot he had been aching to taste since he saw her.

Every time Bernie tried to get up, Gibson's hand would clamp onto her breast, tight and hard, forcing her down so he could continue the incessant, delicious oral torture. He licked her with long, slow motions, nipped her gently with his teeth, and invaded her core with his roughened, expert fingertips until she broke to pieces before him. After he gave her a series of minor orgasms, he was finally ready to move on to another position. He lifted off his knees and looked at her: ravaged, sexed, and hot as hell.

Sitting next to her, he pulled down his shorts as much as her hunger would allow. The minute his sex was exposed, she mounted him, giving a deep, satisfying groan as she stretched to fit him.

Without warning, Gibson thrust into her with more force than he'd ever used on any woman, releasing a feral moan as he did so. His every male instinct ached to be deep inside this pussy, owning it, claiming it with ferocity. Soon, much too soon, his vision flooded with stars and his body shook with violent abandon, and Gibson knew there would not be enough of this woman to satiate his need. Exhausted, he pulled her to him and kissed her deeply.

Hours later, in her bed, he kissed the sweet curve of her neck, tasting the salt from her run and their lovemaking. She shifted slightly, fitting herself closer into his hardness. Gibson often held a woman after sex, but spooning with this woman was foreplay. All she had to do was breathe. He'd been awake an hour, hard just as long. But he was hesitant to wake Bernie, because if he did, there was more than one possible outcome. She could react in a variety of ways: have sex with him again, regret having sex with him at all, or kick him out violently and hate herself for what had happened. Option number one was the only acceptable choice.

Bernie pushed her backside into Gibson. "Hi," she said.

The light was green, and there was nowhere Gibson would rather be. He didn't leave that night or the next two after that. Not a soul interrupted their time together. He inhaled her presence in a way he'd never expected. Between the sheets and the conversations, he saw the woman Bernie truly was. Nothing in his life had prepared him for her.

Bernie retreated from time to time, signs of guilt weighing her spirit. Gibson listened as she explained her devotion to her family. Her children were constantly on her mind, and they would never understand what was happening. She had fought for so long to make their lives happy. Her goal was always to give them the stability of family. A tear escaped her, but before she could wipe it away, Gibson kissed it off her cheek.

"I can make you happy, Bernie. He hurt you. That's why you were here drinking your breakfast."

"It's not about him. My children will never forgive me for destroying their home. Everything I've ever done since I had my first has been to make their lives happy. This will undo it all. You've been so good for me, but you really need to go. Please."

"No. I can't; I won't," he insisted.

"Gib, I can't do this. I was drinking away Christmas because I'm not OK. I'm not good for you or anyone. I'm struggling to be fit for my kids. Don't make this harder for me than it already is." Bernie rolled over, turning away from Gibson and letting the tears fall faster.

"It doesn't have to be complicated. He made his choice. I choose you. I think we can do something with this."

"You don't understand. My kids don't know what's going on, nor will they. You don't have children and can't imagine what the fallout of this would be for the rest of their lives. Please. This was beautiful, but I was drunk and didn't know what I was doing," she said meekly.

"You're kidding me with this shit! You can claim drunk the first day. But you haven't had a drink since. Call it whatever you want, but you were perfectly sober a few hours ago when you fucked me." Gibson rolled away and got out of bed.

He stalked angrily into the shower. After the first afternoon, he had retrieved his vehicle and a duffle bag with fresh clothes. His job as a rigger gave him two weeks off from work, so he had no obligations for a week and a half. That was plenty of time to drink this woman out of his head, he supposed.

He had never even considered living with a woman. That he was even thinking of pursuing this one with three kids and a husband was big—really big—and stupid. He didn't know how, but he would force her off his mind. First, he would wash the smell of her off.

She heard the shower, so she walked straight into the master bath, prepared to do this while he was behind a glass door. As if he'd been about to get her, he stood there. Pulling her in, slamming the door shut, Gibson set her against the wall, his naked body pressed against hers.

"You can't do this to me. How can you pretend this didn't mean something, Bernie?"

"I'm so sorry. It means more than you'll ever know. I want you for me, but I have nothing to offer you. My family is where I belong, whether it's a happy place right now or not."

"If you think you belong to him, you're wrong, babe. Feel this," Gibson said as he pressed hard against her. "Being wanted every minute of the day is something you deserve. You should belong to someone you drive mad just by laughing. I'm fucking obsessed with everything about you. When you said that shit to me, I was on my way to drink and fuck until you were out of my head, but I can't even picture anyone else. I'm ruined."

Then his mouth was on hers, and a careful hand and a powerful thrusting made a closing argument for his case. Gibson took her in the shower before she could try to argue her point. He would screw her into submission. It was the only thing he could think to do to keep her from pushing him away.

—◊◊◊—

According to Bernie, Julian was older than she was. He'd met her when she was a freshman at the university where he was recruiting employees for his firm. The man had quickly proposed marriage. Bernie had wanted to continue dating without the commitment. Within weeks of the rejected proposal, she was pregnant. Every time Bernie went back to college, her contraceptive methods "failed." When she finally graduated, she was six months pregnant with her third child. Julian was the kind of person that could afford a beach house and a European vacation. He could afford a woman like Bernie and a lover. From what Gibson had gathered, this man made a lifestyle of collecting beautiful women while Bernie sat on the shelf. She was more a possession than a partner.

Gibson felt different about Bernie. He could offer her emotional support and a fantastic sex life when he was around, and he would no doubt adore her. Yet, in the back of his mind Gibson understood that he wanted more than sex from this woman—much more.

"I know what you're offering, Julian, but that's not what I need. I needed you to be here. You chose to 'work.' I told you I was leaving, and you told me to do what I had to do!"

Bernie was on the deck, fuming. Julian had finally called. It had been six days, after all. When the phone rang, Bernie had been frantic to find it and leave the house.

The water churned. The air chilled. The conversation stung as Gibson listened to Bernie's side of the conversation from inside the French doors of her beach house.

"No, I won't. I'll go when the kids are on their way. I've spent too many years being the only one trying. You should get your things together and figure out where you'll be sleeping," Bernie raged.

"You wouldn't dare," her husband argued.

In a tone laced with murderous intent but also a calm so scary it revealed that she was fully capable of following through, she said, "You've taken my youth, my happiness, and my patience. You will not have my children. I'll make them orphans before I let that happen."

Bernie spun on her heels toward the doors of the beach house. There she found Gibson smiling. Having heard her side of the conversation, he was sure he had just made enormous progress.

Bernie looked at him in such a way that knocked the smirk off his face. She walked in past the large living area and into the lower-level master bedroom. She went straight to her closet, pulled out a medium-size suitcase, and began packing.

"What are you doing?" Gibson asked. "You just told him you weren't going home."

"I lied." Her stamina died, and she crumpled to the floor is a tearful fit. Gibson came over and tried to embrace her, only to be shoved away.

"Please, leave," Bernie sobbed. "This was a mistake, and I need you out of my life. It's complicated enough as it is."

"Bern—" he tried.

"No. Just go. I can't ever see you again."

Gibson's hurt turned red at the words. He had no need of complications in his life. At almost thirty, he knew he only wanted to work about six months a year. He had a job with a two-week-on / two-week-off schedule. He knew he didn't like owing anyone anything. So he lived in a paid-for sailboat on the marina and owned a paid-for Jeep. He knew he hadn't met anyone for whom he would be willing to give up his lifestyle. This woman was trouble for him. His mind knew that. She had just made the inevitable easier for him.

Gibson grabbed his duffle bag from the floor, aware that he'd left grooming supplies behind in the bathroom. It would serve her well for making him feel this way. He wouldn't be erased from her memory and this place before he hit the road. She was a smart woman with attention to detail. She probably did this kind of thing all the time. His blood ran hotter. The conflict in his mind stabbed him.

What if it was true? What if she did take other lovers? What if she forgot him?

Those thoughts hurt more than they angered him, and that was a really, really bad sign.

In a move that he couldn't even believe he was making, he turned around and came back to where Bernie sat crying on the floor. He helped her up and then violated her mouth with his own until she yielded and neither of them could breathe. When she was limp in his arms, Gibson set her down on the bed. Looking around, he found her cell phone and punched in his contact information.

"You probably won't call me, but here it is anyway. I want you to be part of my life, and even though you don't *want* me in yours right now, I know you need me in it."

The walk to his jeep should not have been so hard, but his legs were heavy and reluctant, weighed down by his damn betraying heart. After serving him well for all these years, the stupid organ had fallen into Bernie's perfectly manicured hands.

Numbing the pain with alcohol and sex was worth a shot, so Gibson went from her beach house to Sharkie's, the closest bar.

It was barely two. The bar was empty . . . until the raven-haired, complicated woman of his dreams sat next to him, ordered a gin and Diet Coke, and smiled.

Gibson knew this was the beginning of the most complicated affair he'd ever been in, but looking at Bernie as she sat next to him was all the encouragement he needed. Bernadine, with a tan line around the most complicated finger, put her small hand on the bar, palm up. Gibson, whose only goal in life had been simplicity, moved his hand from the glass of whiskey and slid his fingers between hers, and that was when he heard the breathe escape her.

 SAFE

Fern Brady

SALIMA MALDONADO AWOKE to the blare of the siren. Her apartment's emergency lighting system switched on as she slid her feet over the side of the bed. The eerie yellow glow emanating from the baseboards cast distorted shadows of her furniture about the room.

"Inspection scan in 10, 9, 8 . . ." The automated voice began the countdown over the speakers.

Salima grabbed the clock on her nightstand. The neon-green numbers told her she could have enjoyed one more hour to sleep before having to start her day. Disgusted at the interruption, she rose and plodded to her kitchen. She pressed her thumb to the reader and switched on the coffee maker, overriding the preset timer.

"Scan in progress," the voice announced.

"Whatever," Salima mumbled, taking a simple white coffee mug down from the cabinet.

At the food dispenser, she placed her palm on the reader. The panel lit up with the touch-screen display. She entered one cup of coffee, and the internal mechanism whirred as the system fetched her allowed sugar packet. Soon the panel door opened. Salima keyed in that she wanted to have bread with butter and orange marmalade for breakfast.

Carbohydrate count too high, the panel display flashed in red. The food dispenser's screen switched, listing three options for breakfast that were approved for her. Salima selected the oatmeal and waited for the necessary ingredients to be placed in the panel door for her. She watched as the system registered the food in her diet journal.

Taking her ingredients back to the counter, she started prepping the oatmeal. Fetching the freshly brewed cup, she added her sugar and stirred absentmindedly.

"Scan complete. Thank you for your cooperation," the computer voice said. The sirens stopped, and the apartment's emergency lighting turned off.

Salima stood in the gray dimness of pre-dawn. The first tenuous rays of the rising sun streamed through the half-open blinds of her windows. Attired in her long, sleeper T-shirt with pictures of cats on it, she sipped her coffee.

"*Meow*," she heard as Miffy jumped up onto the white quartz countertop.

"Hungry, girl?" Salima asked, watching the white ball of fur take a careful seat.

"*Meow*," the cat responded.

Salima returned to the pantry. Activating the reader once more with her palm, she requested the portion for her cat's breakfast. Soon they were both eating their government-approved meals.

After the forced early breakfast, Salima used the bathroom. Once a month, the system attached to the toilet bowl took a random sample of her urine and feces for a health status check. As she flushed, Salima noticed the flashing red light of the analyzer. The computer would use the results of this scan, as well as of the required weekly blood draw, to determine changes to her sanctioned diet.

As annoying as some people found this to be, Salima felt that it made sense. After all, these measures ensured that the population remained in prime health and minimized unnecessary diseases, thus saving the nation and the people a lot of money. Salima felt a sense of pride as each month her health report came back with the seal of *Optimal*.

Getting into the shower, Salima washed her long, brown hair and remembered the conversation she'd had with her grandmother over Thanksgiving a few months back. Nana had been a child when the war broke out that lead to the new government and constitution. She loved to share stories of how things used to be in the United States.

"I still remember the days when we had to go to big stores called supermarkets," her eighty-year-old Nana had told her as they worked in the kitchen of her parents' home in the suburbs of Houston. "You could choose whatever you wanted. Of course, that led to a lot of diseases because people chose fatty or sugary foods. Now, with the new system, it keeps us all healthy."

Stepping from the shower, Salima prepared for her day. She smiled, thinking of how easy life was now. And safe.

—⁕⁕—

Sometime later, Salima checked out of her apartment to head to her job at the bank. The scan assessed her outfit to ensure she was in her work uniform. Taking the elevator down to the second floor, she made her way across the breezeway that connected her building to the platform of the monorail stop.

Her job had been assigned to her because of her high marks in all her math courses. Salima recalled how she had really hoped to be a biologist, but the government's computer determined that being an accountant was the best use for her. So her university studies had been structured for her to hold this job.

She couldn't complain. It was a good job. The One Bank, which was government owned, made sure everyone's digital accounts were accurate. Nana had shown her the old paper money and coins. Salima couldn't believe such an inaccurate system was allowed to exist for so long. Now every dollar was accounted for digitally, and no physical money was needed.

Arriving at work, Salima rode the elevator to the fourth floor, where the "checkers" had their cubicles. The nickname for those who performed her job was ironic, given the office space was laid out in a checkerboard fashion.

"How was your date?" Darlene, her cubicle mate, inquired.

"Pathetic," Salima responded, dropping her hardy messenger bag into its usual drawer.

"I don't understand how they pick these guys," Darlene commented, shaking her head. "The last one I went out with was awful."

"I'm going to get some coffee," Salima stated abruptly. She didn't like talking about the forced dating system the government had implemented ten years back.

In the elegantly appointed kitchen of her floor, Salima brewed herself a cup of coffee and thought about the government's plan to make sure all couplings were successful. In high school, a blood test and an analysis of each person's responses to a visual exam determined if the person was a heterosexual or a homosexual. If the person turned out to be transgender in their responses, the government-approved operation corrected the mistake in gender birth. Salima had rejoiced to know she was indeed a heterosexual female. She'd always thought her math teacher, Mr. Vanderhorn, was hot.

No one was allowed to date until they turned twenty-one. Upon reaching coupling age, Salima was sent potential mate profiles from the main computer. She could decide who to send a date request to, and she had received many. For the first two years, she had rejected all of them. Then she had received the message about her duty to society. She had started going on the occasional date, but really it was just to make sure she stayed on the positive side of the government.

As her coffee finished brewing, she requested a packet of sugar from the food dispenser, but it reminded her that her DNA was prone to diabetes, and it declined. Black, sugarless coffee would have to do. Every day was the same response. Salima couldn't say why she felt compelled to keep asking, but she did.

Back at her cubicle, Salima reconciled the accounts assigned to her to ensure they were accurate. Many thought the position unnecessary. The computer, after all, kept accounting perfectly. But there was still the possibility of hackers, so her job was to reconcile the files sent from individual vendors and employers against the balances of the individual account holders or companies to make sure no one was digitally siphoning away funds.

"You have that look on your face again," Salima heard. His voice sent a thrill down her back. She looked up into the blue-green eyes of her coworker Kyle, who stood leaning over the cubicle's walls.

"What look is that?" she asked, her voice a bit breathless.

He flashed her a smile that brought a surge of heat to her cheeks. "There's this look you get when you're really concentrating on the sums. Your tongue kinda sticks out a little, and you look . . . I don't know . . . lovely." His voice lowered on the last word. He leaned in and whispered. "Why don't we have dinner after work?"

"Yes." The word was out before she had time to really think about the implications.

"Perfect. I'll be by at five." He gave her a wink and walked back across the room to his own cubicle in the high-volume corporate accounts section.

"What are you doing?" Darlene rolled her chair over, her voice a harsh whisper.

"I'm going to enjoy a nice meal with my coworker," Salima whispered back.

"You're going on an unapproved date." Darlene touched her arm and squeezed. "Be careful."

"It'll be OK. Don't worry; it's just dinner."

Concentrating became impossible after that. First, Salima's mind was bombarded by the scenarios that might play out that evening. Worry gnawed at her. She had never personally run afoul of the system. Actually, Salima had no real idea of what happened if you went against the government. No one she knew had ever done anything to warrant government action. But Kyle was hot, in a nerdy kind of way.

Kyle had been among the first to welcome her when she joined the bank two years ago. He would often ride the elevator with her at the end of the day, and he always had something funny to share. He liked the same flavored coffee (hazelnut crème) that she did. After he discovered she was allowed only one sugar packet per day, from time to time he'd drop off a cup at her desk around mid-afternoon.

"This one's sweet," he'd whisper with a wink.

To Salima, it was obvious he liked her. Salima liked him too, but for whatever reason, the system had never matched them. Of course, they had gone to dinner before, though never just the two of them. They had always hung out with other coworkers.

By the end of the day, Salima had concluded that she would just enjoy a nice dinner with a coworker. That's all it would be, even if she did feel attracted to Kyle. She would make sure not to get herself in any kind of trouble.

———〰️———

At five, Kyle stood in front of her cubicle, his backpack over his shoulder and a broad smile wreathed on his face.

"Ready?" he asked.

"Yep." Salima yanked her messenger bag from the drawer and threw it over her head so the strap clung across her body. "Where are we going?"

"Do you like Asian food?"

"Love it!" she said.

"How about PF Chang's, then?"

"Works for me!" Salima briefly considered turning to Darlene and inviting her along. That would make it a coworker get-together. But the thrill of being alone with Kyle kept her from doing so. *Cool your head*, she told herself.

They walked to the elevators, riding down to the second floor in silence, squished between other bank employees heading home after the day's work. They crossed the breezeway to the stop of the monorail. Eventually they boarded the line that would take them toward the restaurant.

"So, how do you like working at the bank?" Salima asked, trying to start a conversation.

"It's all right," Kyle responded. He leaned his shoulder into hers as he continued, "I had hoped to go into the sciences, but my scores gave me this assignment. How about you?"

"Me too!" Salima responded. "I wanted to be a biologist. Study animals and work with them."

"Really? I had thought of geology. I really love reading and learning about volcanoes and the geologic record."

They settled into amicable chatter about the various scientific developments that fascinated them. Before they knew it, the rail was drawing up at their stop.

When they stepped into the foyer of the restaurant, savory aromas greeted them. There were a few people already seated on the sofa benches waiting for tables.

"Welcome to PF Chang's," the automated greeter announced. "Please check in, and we will show you to your table shortly."

Kyle put his palm on the scanner. It brought up his picture, and he keyed in their purpose: coworker dinner. Then Salima placed her palm on the scanner.

A waitress opened the door at the other end of the enclosed space and called out the name of the next party. All four people seated there stood to follow her, leaving Salima and Kyle alone.

"So, what kind of accounts do you mostly handle?" Salima asked, wanting to make the conversation as work related as possible in case it was being monitored. She had heard that public conversations could be recorded for national security purposes. Banks of computer servers were said to analyze billions of conversations fed randomly for key phrases that might indicate a threat to the safety of the United States and its people.

"I do a lot of big corporate accounts," Kyle said. "You know, I received a commendation for my work last quarter. I think they may ask me to take the executive position that Mr. Baker will vacate when he retires in a couple months."

"Oh, how exciting!" Salima tried to sound genuinely happy for him, though it would mean he would move up to the top floors. It was likely she would never see him again after that. Execs didn't mingle with the accounting people.

"Yeah." Kyle's face lit up, and he added, "I'd get to have a car then."

"That would be so nice," Salima commented wistfully.

"Oh, yeah!" Kyle took out his phone and showed her a few cars he hoped would be viable options for him. "I really don't understand why we can't all have cars."

"Coworker dinner party?" the waitress called from the door.

They followed her through the restaurant to a comfortable booth. Once seated, they took their turn placing their palm onto the reader, which selected from the restaurant's menu the options that would work with their prescribed diets.

"Don't you wish you could just order whatever you wanted?" Kyle commented after they made their selections.

"Well, this helps our economy." Salima felt obligated to defend the system. "After all, ever since they implemented the new constitution after the war, we have fewer sick people, which means fewer expenses for the health insurances and systems. Also, with only the executive level and higher people using cars, there is less traffic, less road-rage violence, and—"

"Yes, yes, of course," Kyle said, waving a dismissive hand. "The post-war constitution helped create a society in which we are all safe."

"As much as possible," Salima said.

An awkward silence fell on their table. Salima felt sad that the warm comradery of their earlier conversation had fallen apart.

"Do you have pets?" she asked.

"I'm not allowed pets," Kyle responded. "My DNA indicates a propensity for allergies related to pet dander."

"Ah." Salima didn't know what to say, so she decided to let him take over trying to converse.

After a moment, he asked, "Do you have pets?"

"I have a cat," she replied.

"Why not a dog?"

"Well, sometimes I have to stay late at work, and a cat is more independent," Salima explained her decision-making process. "Mostly, I think I didn't want to have to walk it every day or have to take it outside to do its business. Cats are less maintenance, I think."

"Makes sense."

Their food arrived, and the conversation flow improved as they discussed the flavors of the meal they had each chosen.

"Would you like a drink?" Kyle asked. "I still have my allotment for the week."

"Um . . . yes. That would be nice."

Kyle placed his palm on the reader. He selected a twisted whiskey sour. Salima tried to order an Asian pear mojito, but the sugar content was too high. She tried a Chang's Mai Tai but was declined again.

"Try the spiked lemon tea," Kyle suggested. "It has the least amount of alcohol in it."

That one was approved. The conversation turned to favorite foods, movies, and books. Salima discovered that Kyle's taste matched her own in almost everything. She wondered if they could request to be paired together. Would he like that idea?

As the evening continued, they tried to order a second drink. Both were declined.

"Don't know why," Kyle commented. "Neither of us is driving."

"Well, alcoholism was a big problem, and—"

"Yes, Salima. We are protected this way." His tone spoke the contempt he had for the system that kept their society safe. "Don't you ever wish you could just do what you want, whenever you want?"

"Of course," Salima said with a shrug of her slender shoulders. "But that kind of thing lead to all kinds of problems, which landed us in wars. This way, well, we're safe."

"I suppose you're right." Kyle paid for the meal. "Shall we?"

They headed out into the warm and muggy Houston summer night.

"I had a very lovely evening," Salima commented when they once again stood at the monorail stop.

"Me too." Kyle took her hand to help her step up onto the public transport unit. She felt a shiver of guilty pleasure as his fingers ran across her skin. "I'll see you home, if that's OK."

"Yes," Salima responded, wondering if it was wise to let him do so. "That would be nice."

Kyle saw her all the way to the door of her apartment. They stood there for a moment, uncertain how to end the evening.

"Want some coffee?" Salima heard herself say, though she wasn't sure the system would approve a fourth cup this late, with work on the morrow. It might be too much caffeine.

Kyle flashed her a flirty smile. "Love some."

She placed her palm on the reader, and her apartment door unlocked. He entered behind her and stood gazing about her small abode. Salima had already headed to the kitchen when the alarm began to blare and the emergency lighting replaced the soft light of her lamps.

"Unauthorized visitor. Please check in," the computer voice commanded.

Kyle went over to the palm reader and checked in as "friend." The alarm silenced, and the lighting went back to normal.

"Geez!" Kyle laughed, leaning on the countertop. Salima joined in his mirth.

And then she was in his arms, and he was kissing her. The feel of his lips on hers sent a shiver of desire through her body.

"Wait," she managed to whisper as his mouth rained kisses down her neck. "We are not—"

Kyle silenced her with a deep, hungry kiss. His hands trailed over her, eager to explore. Salima felt warmth pool in her abdomen. He pressed his body into hers as he positioned her up against the countertop. She wrapped herself around him, returning his kisses with a matching hunger.

Her mind told her to stop; it warned that this was not approved. But her mind was overcome by the longing of her body. Salima had never been with a man. Every caress of his strong hands, each kiss of his lips made her skin catch fire.

They ripped their clothing off each other, making their way clumsily to her bed. Between hot, passionate kisses, they giggled at their awkwardness.

It was the most glorious moment of Salima's whole life.

—⁓—

Hours later, Salima awoke alone and naked in her bed. She glanced at the clock. It read three in the morning. She vaguely wondered what time Kyle left. Would there be a problem? Would the system know that they had been together?

She knew that once approved to couple with a mate, he underwent the reversible sterilization process. This ensured childbearing came once the relationship was economically prepared for it. Kyle surely wasn't sterilized.

Because all couplings were strictly controlled, condoms, which in the pre-war era served as protection during sexual encounters, had been banned. The fear of an unapproved pregnancy and of the government interventions for unauthorized couplings kept most of the people in line. Neither Salima, nor any of her friends, had ever dared to test the system. Until tonight.

The sudden vivid idea that she might be pregnant flashed in her mind. She touched her belly with a gentle hand. Would she be allowed to keep the baby if she was? Abortions had been all but done away with now that the government had firm control of couplings. Would a random scan show the computer that there had been a mating? They had already scanned the apartment that morning. Another scan wasn't due for at least a month, but from time to time they scanned back to back—to keep people on their toes, she guessed. She decided she should get up and replace her sheets. She quickly threw the used sheets into the small-stacked washing machine unit and dressed the bed with a clean set.

Lying there, unable to return to sleep, Salima relived the delicious sensations that lingered over her body from their lovemaking. She moved her hands over where he had caressed her. She breathed in the scent of their mating that yet tinged the apartment. Eventually she drifted off to sleep again.

The next day, Salima arrived to work at her usual hour, dropped her messenger bag in her drawer, and headed to the office kitchen for her second cup of unsweetened coffee. The day's work waited for her in her inbox. She glanced around to Kyle's cubicle, but he wasn't in yet.

"Come with me!" the command startled her from the row of numbers she had been verifying.

"What?" Looking up, confused, Salima noticed it had only been about fifteen minutes since she'd checked in. The office was mostly empty, as most workers came in right at nine o'clock, which was still about a half hour away.

"Come. With. Me." The man in the police uniform repeated the words slowly as if she were dimwitted.

"OK." Salima rose from her chair and got her bag from her drawer.

"I'll take that." The officer yanked it away from her before she could utter a protest.

Salima followed him to the bank of elevators, peeking quickly to see if Kyle was at his desk. He wasn't. She caught Darlene's concerned look as she passed her cubicle mate, who was disembarking the elevator as Salima and the guard boarded.

"Where are we going?" Salima asked once they were alone in the elevator and heading to the basement level. "May I ask what I did wrong?"

"You will be told soon enough." The officer stood stoically, Salima's messenger bag dangling from his clenched hands.

They turned right when the elevator doors opened. He led the way down white-walled hallways that twisted and turned like a never-ending labyrinth. Eventually they came to a wider area with a desk next to a stainless-steel door. Another officer sat there.

The one guiding her placed his palm on the door reader, and the door opened for him. She was instructed to check in on the reader. It registered her identity but didn't ask what purpose she had there. He gave her a shove to proceed, and the door clicked shut behind her.

Opening a door to their left, he revealed a small room. "Sit here," he instructed. "Someone will be with you shortly." Once she stepped inside, he left her there, the lock clicking shut as it closed behind him.

Salima sat on the cold gray metal chair. She placed her hands on the cold square metal table. She realized the officer had kept her bag, but all she could do was sit, anguished as to what was about to happen. She had always known that the bottom floors were for security. A shiver of dread shook her as she waited haplessly in what was clearly an interrogation room. She had no idea how much time passed.

The door finally opened, and two women entered. One dressed in a perfectly tailored navy-blue skirt suit bearing a gold name badge on her lapel. The other was in a white lab coat. She held a tray with a syringe, a rubber string band, and a couple vials for blood sample collection.

"Salima Maldonado," the lady in the blue suit said, sitting down across from her and setting a file on the table. "I'm Health Enforcement Special Agent Marge White. We will need to take some blood so we can make the final determination as to your options in this situation. May we?"

"Yes." Salima's voice was barely a whisper. Her heart pounded, and sweat dampened her palms. Fear constricted her throat. A health enforcement agent meant this was about last night—about what Kyle and she had shared.

"You don't need to worry," HESA Marge reassured, nodding to the lab lady to proceed. "What you and Kyle have done is ill advised, but we will be able to work it out. It isn't like you are criminals or anything." She smiled then, as if that should make Salima feel all better.

It didn't.

The lab lady took the samples, leaving the room once she had enough of Salima's blood.

HESA Marge opened the file she had placed on the table. "I see here that you and Kyle went on an unapproved date, masquerading it as a coworker dinner. Everything would have been ignored, but the system recorded that he entered your apartment, initially without checking in, at 9:30 and did not leave until just before 3 a.m. Is that correct?"

"I don't know what time he left," Salima found herself whispering in answer.

"You coupled?"

It wasn't really a question. They already knew she had been with Kyle. Salima's eyes swam with tears. She wanted to hold herself together, to be strong, but instead she began sobbing uncontrollably.

"There now," HESA Marge said, moving to sit in a chair next to Salima. She placed a hand on Salima's shoulders as she continued, "It will be all right. This is not a crime. It can be fixed and, who knows, perhaps you will be allowed to become life mates. The blood tests will tell us what your options are."

Salima struggled to pull herself together. The lab-coat lady returned and placed a Kleenex box in front of Salima, who took fistfuls.

"Calm yourself," Marge instructed with less empathy and more authority. "Now, we will bring Kyle in and discuss this reasonably."

She moved to the spot she had occupied across the table at first. The door opened, and Kyle was ushered in by a man in a perfectly tailored suit identical in style and color to HESA Marge's suit. Salima met Kyle's blue-green eyes. He flashed her his broad smile, coming to sit beside her in the chair that HESA Marge had vacated. The suited man sat down beside HESA Marge, while the lab-coat lady closed the door behind her.

"Are you OK?" Kyle asked Salima, taking her hand.

"She is fine," HESA Marge answered before Salima could utter a word. "Now, as it turns out, the reason the two of you were never suggested for each other by the master computer is that, genetically, there is the potential that a child born from the two of you will have serious mental defects."

Salima stared at her in shock. She turned to Kyle, who stared at their entwined hands resting on his knee.

"I'm Health Enforcement Special Agent John Hagen, Salima. Kyle and I have been talking about some options you two have. If you are interested in becoming life mates, we can offer you that opportunity," HESA John stated evenly. "Provided, of course, that you, Salima, agree to permanent sterilization. We can't risk burdening society with a mentally defective birth."

"It isn't for sure our child would be born with a defect," Kyle protested. "It's just a—"

"It is a chance society is not willing to take." HESA Marge's tone brooked no argument.

After an awkward silence, HESA Marge stood, signaling HESA John. "We will let you discuss this option. Kyle, you and HESA John have reviewed the outcome should you decide not to mate. It is your choice."

They left. The click of the door sounded loud in the silence of the room. Salima stared down at her hand in Kyle's. She had no idea what to say.

"So," Kyle began, releasing her hand and pulling on her chair so that they faced each other. Salima locked eyes with him as he continued. "If you and I wish to be together, then we can. We can be life mates. We won't be allowed to have children, but we can enjoy our lives together. I will be given the executive position, and if I perform well, I might someday be promoted to partnership level. That would allow us access to genetic child production. So, we might have a baby down the road."

He stared at her with hopeful eyes. She could feel him willing her to agree to this. Salima's mind reeled with the information.

"Of course, if you don't want to, that's OK." She watched as he rubbed his hands on his knees and avoided her gaze. "In that case, I will be moved to the San Antonio office. To avoid, you know . . . awkwardness."

"But what about the executive promotion here?" Salima blurted out.

"Nah." Kyle looked at her then. His eyes filled with sadness and longing. "I wouldn't be able to get that. They don't want us in the same city if we have this strong of an attraction."

"Oh." Salima felt a sudden oppression on her chest. His fate depended on her choice.

The small room was suffocatingly constricting. Her mind turned over the options. If she mated with Kyle, she would be sterilized. They might have a baby, assuming he reached the partner level. At that level, they could have their ova and sperm genetically reworked to ensure no defects in the baby. That option wasn't a guarantee. But it was a possibility, and Kyle was a hard worker and smart.

Salima had never really felt like being with anyone. Kyle was the only one who had ever made her feel comfortable enough to talk freely and to dream of—

"Don't feel pressured, Salima," Kyle spoke, breaking through her thoughts. "If you don't want to be with me forever . . . it is a long time . . . don't feel you have to." He scooted up to the edge of his chair and took her hands in his. "I will take the transfer. I can work just as hard over there. Sooner or later I'll make it to the executive level. I—"

"Kyle," Salima started to say through dry lips, but he interrupted.

"From the moment you joined the company, I couldn't take my eyes off you. All I could think is how beautiful you are, how smart, how funny. I found every way I could to bump into you and talk to you. I did that until I just needed to ask you out. I did this to us! I am sorry, Salima." His eyes teared up. "I didn't . . ."

Salima hugged him then. She didn't want him to feel bad. Not after the beauty of what they had shared. He hugged her back, crying into her chest as they tumbled off the chairs to sit awkwardly on the cold, hard floor.

"I'll be your life mate, Kyle," Salima whispered into his ear. "You're the only one I've ever wanted to be with too."

—⁓—

HESA Marge and HESA John returned to the room when Kyle knocked on the locked door.

"You've made your choice, then?" HESA John inquired.

"We want to be life mates," Kyle announced for them, standing close to Salima and holding her hand.

"Come with me, Salima," HESA Marge commanded.

Kyle held her hand tighter. "Where are you taking her?"

"While you and John fill out the paperwork, I will take Salima to the clinic. She will need to be cleansed from the possible results of your night together." HESA Marge extended a hand to Salima.

Salima felt a new shiver of dread run down her spine. But she felt Kyle tensing, and she wished to keep things civil. They had messed up. Better to just deal with whatever consequences were left to go through.

"I'll be OK," Salima turned to Kyle, reassuring him. "You fill out the papers. We'll be together." She felt him let go reluctantly.

Salima followed HESA Marge into the hall. Exiting the security wing, they turned toward the clinic end of the basement level. Salima was familiar with this area, as she made her monthly visit for check-ups with Dr. Florence there as required by bank policy.

HESA Marge led her past the people in the waiting room to a chamber in the back. Dr. Florence, accompanied by Nurse Jane, waited for her there.

"I'll leave you in their hands," HESA Marge stated. "After the procedure, you will be sent home. It is best you rest. Tomorrow is Saturday, so you'll have the weekend to recuperate, though I understand there should be no after effects."

"You'll have cramping," Dr. Florence told her once she had undressed and was on the table. "They say no effects, but you'll have cramping, my dear. We'll give you some meds to make it better, though."

Nurse Jane gave her an injection to numb her lower abdomen. Then the cleansing began.

Salima lay on her bed crying. It hadn't hurt. At first, she had felt cramping, but the pain med kicked in an hour ago, so she felt no physical discomfort.

But she cried.

She cried about the embarrassment of being there, spread-eagle. She cried about the feelings of horror as she realized what they were doing to "cleanse" her. Salima had asked if there wasn't a pill or some other way. She was informed that the government required this in order to ensure there would be no mistake.

Now Salima wondered if she was making the right choice mating with Kyle. Before leaving the clinic, Dr. Florence set her appointment for sterilization.

"It won't be right away," he'd explained. "Closer to the Life-Commitment ceremony. It's a permanent procedure, and you have to be really sure."

Salima's mind pondered what would be done to her in six months' time. No uterus. No baby. How would she tell her parents they would possibly never have a grandchild? Sobs wracked her body. She curled herself into a ball.

Miffy had been rehomed. Salima's apartment was purified. Kyle couldn't have pets. She would never be able to bother her white puff of fur by hugging him again. No baby. No pets. Salima buried her face into her tear-drenched pillow.

A sudden weight on the bed startled Salima. Turning, she saw Kyle in the dim light of sunset that managed to penetrate the tightly closed blinds of her room.

"It's me," he said unnecessarily. "They let me have access now. I was given the temporary sterilization today."

He knelt there on the edge of her bed. Salima sat up. They stared at each other awkwardly.

"Are you OK?" Kyle asked.

"I will be," Salima asserted.

He reached for her. She curled into his arms. They lay there together in silence for a time. Then they started making plans for their future. He would meet her parents. She would meet his. They would be given a bigger apartment. Life would be good.

Yes, Salima thought as she fell asleep at last in his arms, they would be happy together.

～◎ SHE LOVES ME, SHE LOVES ME NOT ◎＜

J. Dennis Papp

WHEN ROSE MARIE WATSON and Carter Carr reached simultaneously for the lone pair of pastry tongs, a spark shot out of their combined effort. They both flinched.

"Must have been static electricity," Carter said. "From the rug."

Rose Marie looked into Carter's hazel eyes and immediately became entranced. It was as though they were the portal to his soul, and she viewed a spirit rich in tenderness and warmth. The impression that she knew this man—maybe in another life?—flooded her senses, making her believe "static electricity" had nothing to do with what they shared.

"Static electricity. *Riiight*," she agreed.

Carter, ever the gentleman, offered his hand in a friendly greeting and introduced himself. When Rose Marie accepted the gesture, no sparks flew. However, both *were* charged by their simple contact, heightening their immediate charisma for each other. Neither had ever experienced an attraction that transcended the physical.

"So what brought you here?" Rose Marie asked.

They were attending a murder-mystery weekend at a convention center in picturesque Princeton, New Jersey. Guests were helping themselves to the refreshments, exchanging the usual introductory small talk.

"I'm a native Londoner and relocated recently to the colonies," he smiled. His neatly trimmed brown hair gently caressed his broad shoulders as it fluttered in the breeze created by the heating system. "With Sherlock Holmes infused in every neighborhood of my city, I became an instant mystery buff." Another beacon from his face lit up the room. "What about you?"

"I got the mystery bug as a teenager when I first entered the adult's room at my local library. One look at a bookshelf full of novels, with skulls and crossbones on their spines, was all it took to get hooked on the genre," she said.

"So it had nothing to do with your last name being *Watson*?" Carter asked.

She frowned and shook her head.

Several of the male guests gathered around the refreshments table, crowding out Carter. They made a point of facing Rose Marie. The frontal approach afforded the best view of her generous breasts, which were partially visible through a peek-a-boo pink blouse. Although Rose Marie had recently celebrated her forty-fifth birthday, she still looked damned good in spite of having some extra sand in her hourglass figure.

In another cluster of guests, mainly women, one man excused himself from the conversation and walked toward the podium. His clothing resembled that of a butler's. If everyone would take a seat," Nick Kris said, the microphone accentuating his deep voice, "we can get started."

Carter Carr helped Rose Marie with her chair, making sure to take the one to Rose Marie's left. The "wrong way" women's blouses buttoned, Carter believed, always made the left side the best place to sit next to a woman. That, of course, was if the view was worth the trouble. And with Rose Marie, he was willing to crawl through a mile of broken glass to view the Promised Land.

Rose Marie leaned over and whispered into Carter's right ear: "Besides having a charming English accent, you're quite the gentleman." She squeezed his right forearm and let her hand linger.

Carter, unable to vocalize a thank-you, because his heart had just taken up residence in his throat, simply smiled. While inhaling her cherry-blossom fragrance, he made a conscious effort to keep his eyes in his head with the even-better view Rose Marie gave him with her leaning-over compliment. Rose Marie caught Carter's sheepish glance when it traveled from paradise to her face. She winked in recognition. His cheeks flushed. He tugged on his collar to release some of the built-up steam.

Nick Kris went through the basics on how events would transpire for the murder-mystery weekend. A light meal followed his presentation, and the guests began leaving their tables.

"Well, I guess that's it for tonight," Rose Marie said to Carter.

When they exchanged the expected handshake, sparks again jolted their arms.

"It d-doesn't have to be," Carter stammered, as blood rushed from his brain to another body part. "H-how about an after-dinner drink in the lounge?"

When Rose Marie lowered her glance, she blushed at his swollen manhood. "Well, sure. But just one. OK?"

Lost for words, Carter simply nodded.

—◆—

One drink became two. A pleasant glow came over Rose Marie and Carter, intensifying the emotional attraction between them. Instead of a third drink, their eyes expressed their intense physical desire and an interest in continuing their glow elsewhere. They gravitated to Carter's room.

He closed the door and blurted out "This has never happened to me before, Rose Marie." His index finger outlined her lips. "Sure, I've made love on a first date. All of twice," he blushed. "But it was with someone I'd known for a long time. A *very* long time."

She kissed his fingertip and smiled.

"But never with anyone I'd just met." He continued to outline her lips. "I've never felt such an immediate attraction to someone." He traced a course to her right cheek. "Such a *strong* attraction. The first time I saw you, I thanked God for the wonderful gift of sight." He brushed away a tear before it completed its trip down her cheek. "I know that sounds like what you Americans would call corny, but it's the truth." He kissed the top of her forehead. "Please believe me."

"I do, Carter. And I have a confession too." She exhaled deeply. "I'm married."

Carter's jaw bounced off his knees. Before he could utter a word, she continued.

"Technically." Rose Marie gazed at the ceiling for inspiration. "My husband and I are separated." *Twenty years down the drain*, she thought. "What once was a marriage is over." *Twenty loving years gone. I forgave him for an indiscretion when we were engaged. But his affair six months ago was too much.* "That's another reason why I came to this murder-mystery weekend. To get away and have some space to think."

"Would you prefer just to sit and talk, instead of—"

Rose Marie's thoughts turned to making love with someone on their first encounter. Something that never before happened. Granted, she had "been" with maybe half a dozen men in her time, but never so fast. Never with such urgency. She answered his question by unbuttoning her pink blouse and letting it fall to the floor.

Carter stepped back and stared at her beckoning cleavage. The air between them almost crackled with electricity. He uttered a simple "mmm" while caressing her with eager fingertips. Rose Marie reached behind her back for her bra.

Continuing to be the gentleman, Carter swallowed a "Here; let me." He slowly undid the four hooks. He punctuated each success by kissing the nape of Rose Marie's neck. Reciprocating, she nibbled his neck while unbuttoning his shirt. In time, each obstacle to ecstasy melted away.

Carter helped Rose Marie pull back the down comforter, revealing the red satin sheets on the waterbed.

"You have a room with a *waterbed*?"

"It only cost a few extra dollars," he smiled. "Thought I'd splurge."

Before joining her in bed, Carter reached into a drawer, extracted two foil packets, and placed them on the night table.

"Oh my God!" Rose Marie shouted, looking down at him.

"What?" Carter asked, abruptly halting the roller-coaster ride.

"Sorry," she whispered, returning his hands to her hips. "It was my way of saying that was absolutely amazing."

"That so?" he asked, smiling. He glanced at the remaining foil packet on the night table. "Want to see if we can improve perfection?"

Rose Marie reached behind her hips and gently squeezed his testicles with her right hand. "Want to live to try another day?" she asked, easing herself off of him.

Carter held up his hands in surrender.

With arms encircled, Rose Marie and Carter lay side by side, basking in the afterglow of physical and emotional release. Their conversation spoke of happiness, pleasure, and the gratitude of a chance encounter that brought them together. Eventually there were longer pauses between Rose Marie's responses. Her thoughts turned to her feelings toward her husband. Did she react too quickly when she told him to pack up and leave *immediately*, after learning of his affair? Should she have given him a last-chance ultimatum instead? Was she partly to blame?

Carter, wide awake, let Rose Marie drift off to sleep as he mentally replayed their lovemaking. Within moments, a gentle awakening in his loins made him wish Rose Marie weren't asleep.

At the conclusion of the murder-mystery weekend—Rose Marie guessed "who-dunit"—the two of them went their separate ways: Rose Marie to her apartment a few miles away in suburban Trenton and Carter to his condo in Newark. They vowed to meet again. Soon.

True to their promise, they got together over the next few weeks for a meal or a movie. They did not make love. Not even once.

Following their fourth date, Carter wanted to rekindle the spark they felt when they first touched—and make love again. Undecided whether he should call her before he changed his mind, he paced from one end of his living room to the other, making round trip after round trip. When he passed the coffee table for the fifth time, he stopped suddenly and stared at his cell phone. Reaching for it with his left hand, he stopped in mid-air, continuing to stare at it.

Do it, you bloody fool, he told himself. *Pick up the damned mobile and ring her up.*

He closed his eyes and mentally inhaled Rose Marie's cherry-blossom perfume. The deeper he inhaled, the closer she felt. He could see her standing before him, only a few feet away. The delicious contours of her body. The outline of her angel-wing-shaped lips, which tasted as good as they looked. Carter unconsciously raised his arms to embrace her, fighting off the urge to cup his eager hands around her overflowing breasts. He took two steps forward. Reaching for her image—

Ring! Ring!

Startled, Carter dropped his cell. His eyes flew open. The vision of Rose Marie melted away.

Ring! Ring!

He rescued the phone from the floor. "Hello?" he said.

Ring! Ring!

Wondering why it was still ringing, he had an epiphany. "It's the bloody *land-line*," he said to no one in particular.

Ring! Ring!

Grabbing the extension in the living room, he barked: "Hello?"

"I'd like to speak with Carter Carr."

It was a woman's voice. Could it be Rose Marie? Could he have telepathically reached out to her? No. It couldn't be. He never gave her his home phone number—just his mobile. So, who was calling him?

"Speaking."

"Mr. Carr, this is Joan Linden. How are you today?" Before Carter could say anything, Linden continued. "I'm glad to hear that, Mr. Carr. I'm calling from

Verizon with a wonderful money-saving offer on your long-distance calls, Mr. Carr."

Bloody hell! Carter thought. "I'm not interested. Thank you."

"But you *must* be interested in saving money, Mr. Carr. I know you are, Mr. Carr. That's why I'm calling with this special offer, Mr. Carr. So you'll switch to Verizon, Mr. Carr."

"I'm already—"

"Which long-distance carrier do you have now, Mr. Carr? I know you can't be happy with their service, Mr. Carr. Or with the cost. Are you, Mr. Carr? That's why I'm—"

"Look, you bloody idiot," Carter barked, fighting back the urge to use stronger language because he *did* have Verizon. "I already have—"

"That's OK, Mr. Carr. You don't have to tell me who you have, Mr. Carr. Because I just know they can't be as good as us, Mr. Carr."

"I already have Verizon!" he yelled into the receiver.

"Well, good, Mr. Carr. And I know you're happy you chose us, Mr. Carr. Now I want to make you even happier, Mr. Carr, by offering—"

"The only way I can be happier is if I do this."

"Do what, Mr. Carr?"

Carter grinned and slammed down the phone.

—ᴧᴧ—

Rose Marie unscrewed the "R" cap on the contact lens storage case and eased the lens onto her right palm. After rinsing off the multi-purpose solution with saline, she guided the contact onto her left index finger. Using her right thumb and index finger to hold open her upper and lower eyelids, she tapped the lens onto the eyeball and blinked. After a second blink, the right eye slid into focus, the blurriness disappearing.

With both lenses now in place, Rose Marie applied a modest amount of makeup and exited the bathroom.

She selected an appropriate business outfit from her closet and dropped it on the bed. Although she dressed conservatively for work, she had a few provocative outfits that exposed and clung to the *right* parts of her queen-sized figure. She smiled at the thought of wearing one for Carter.

Before leaving the bedroom, she checked her appearance in the mirror— not so much to admire herself but to take pride in her appearance. After all, she reasoned, a woman didn't have to be model-thin to be attractive. As she held her breath and buttoned her blouse, commonsense told her it wouldn't hurt to lose a *few* pounds. Searching her purse for her keys, the telephone rang.

"Hello?"

"Rose Marie, it's Tom."

Her husband. *What did he want now?* she wondered.

"I don't have time to talk now; I'll be late for work," she responded, knowing full well she had at least fifteen minutes to spare. "Today's Friday, and I have a lot to get done before the week's over."

"Look. We need to talk. I've been a fool—"

"Damned right, you have!" she shouted.

"Please let me—"

"I can't talk now." *I really don't want to* was what she actually wanted to say. *Even though I may have acted too impulsively when I demanded that you leave immediately.* "I don't want to discuss this over the phone. And anyway, I've got to go. Bye."

———〜〜〜———

During the short drive to work, Rose Marie wondered if she should have talked with Tom. Should she give two decades of marriage another chance? She had taken Tom back once before, while they were engaged, and nothing seemed to have changed with his behavior. Was Carter the solution to her problems? She was so immersed in thought that she drove past her office building. Pulling into a nearby lot, she turned around and corrected her error.

"Good morning, Rose Marie."

"Morning, Suzie."

"You look a little distracted," commented her assistant. "Is everything OK?"

"Just have something on my mind. Nothing major." *"Nothing major" my butt. Just my marriage and the rest of my life.*

Not twenty minutes after Rose Marie sat behind her desk, the phone rang. She looked out her office door to see if Suzie would answer it, but her assistant was not in sight. Hoping it wasn't her husband trying her at work, Rose Marie picked up her phone and gave a hesitant greeting.

"This is Rose Marie. How may I help you?"

"Good morning, gorgeous. I can think of several ways you can help me."

It was Carter—thank God. Rose Marie couldn't help but smile at his thought pattern.

"How are you today?" he asked. Not getting an instant response from her, he asked, "You OK?"

Trying to sound positive, she eventually replied, "Couldn't be better."

"Great. I was wondering if you'd like to go to brunch on Sunday. I saw an advertisement for a nice place down your way and figured we could give it a try."

"OK. Sure. Sounds good," came her staccato response.

Breaking the connection, Rose Marie hoped there wouldn't be another phone call from a man—the one she regretted getting.

———

"I'm glad you talked me into coming back to my apartment after brunch," Rose Marie said, turning on a dimmer switch. "And thanks for these lovely flowers. Where did you find daisies this time of year?" A brass floor lamp came gradually to life, creating a glow in one corner of the living room.

"I have my sources," Carter smiled, glad that she was in a much better mood than when he had called her on Friday.

Rose Marie touched a button, and music softly filled the room. After lighting a strawberry-scented candle, she turned and faced Carter.

———

After their lovemaking, feeling himself go limp, he withdrew from the warmth deep inside her. Rolling over on his back, he wrapped an arm around her.

"There's nothing better than making love on a snowy afternoon," he said, brushing his lips along her neck. "On *any* afternoon." He looked down at Rose Marie, feeling her smile before he saw it. *So this is what intimacy truly is?* he thought. He smiled back. *I'm so glad I found you, Rose Marie Watson.* "What a wonderful way to begin a week," he added, his cupped hand finding a breast. "I love Sunday afternoons with you, Rose Marie."

"Mmm," she said. "Me, too."

"Oh? You love Sunday afternoons with *yourself*?" he kidded.

"No, silly." She flicked her middle finger at his wilted, condom-covered penis. "With you."

"Hey, watch it. You'll break the darned thing with your nail," he cautioned jokingly.

"I didn't know your *thing* was so delicate."

"Not my pecker; the rubber." He squeezed her breast. "Don't want my whatchamacallits swimming all over the sheets."

"Sorry," she said, pulling on the tip of the condom and letting it snap back. "We couldn't have that," she teased. "At least not in my bed, anyway." Carter repositioned the swollen condom. "Your bed, I don't care about."

"Oh?" Carter said, sitting up.

This time Rose Marie yanked on the condom, pulling it off halfway.

———

Days later, having completed an umpteen-course meal at an excellent Portuguese restaurant in the Ironbound section of Newark, he braved the near-freezing temperature and scurried the few blocks to his condo. Although winter in New Jersey, much to his dismay, meant staying inside to elude the constant snow and the icy wind that blew from every direction, Carter periodically abandoned the hermit mentality to roam the neighborhood. He especially enjoyed the tempting fragrances of the ethnic delicacies all around him. After inhaling untold eclectic flavors on his way home, Carter was thawing out in his living room.

With a snifter of brandy at his side and CNN providing the background diversion, he opened a rosewood humidor and extracted a Marsh Wheeling cigar. He clipped off the pointed end of the cigar—rather than biting it off, Bret Maverick style—and held a flame to it. Exhaling a cloud of blue smoke toward the ceiling, he picked up *The Star-Ledger.* Flipping past the sports section with numerous articles on the just-completed Super Bowl game—*the bloody Americans call* this *football?*—he came to the travel pages. A large ad about the Sunshine State told of the wonders of various vacation spots. The blurb about Orlando caught his eye, especially spending several days in Disney World. The special low airfares for the remainder of February were the clincher.

Thinking that spending two weeks in the sun with Rose Marie would be a great way to warm up—*along with other ways,* he smiled—he decided the trip would be a the main topic of conversation when they next met.

———

"I have a little surprise for you, Rose Marie."

She put down her coffee cup and asked, "What is it?"

"How would you like to escape this cold weather for two weeks?"

She looked out the restaurant window, saw dirty-brown slush that once had been pristine-white snow, and sighed. "I'd love it."

"Then go with me to Orlando."

This was a big step for their relationship. Granted, they had been intimate on many occasions, but had never been away together. Not counting their murder-mystery weekend, of course. A trip for such a length of time would divulge a lot about their compatibility. If things worked out, Tom could be a thing of the past—forever.

"I've seen some all-inclusive packages mentioned in the newspaper. Several include five or seven days in Disney World."

"That sounds like it would be fun."

"And it's just a short flight there," Carter added.

"Oh."

"What's the matter?"

"I don't like to fly," Rose Marie confessed, "especially during the uncertain weather in the winter."

Not to be shot down, Carter suggested taking the train. "We could get a nice compartment all to ourselves," he said smiling, "and enjoy a leisurely overnight trip there."

Rose Marie contemplated her husband's recent phone call, wondering what was on his mind. Figuring nothing would come of a brief exchange of words, she leaned toward escaping with Carter—even if it were for only two weeks.

"Let me think about it until tomorrow. *While I ponder the dilemma of getting back together with my husband.* "OK?"

"Just don't wait more than a day, please. I need time to make the reservations."

—⚬⚬⚬—

The next day, as promised, Rose Marie called Carter and confirmed their trip.

"I prayed that you would, because I made the reservations this morning."

"That was rather presumptuous of you, Carter," she replied in as stern a voice she could contrive.

"I'd rather say *hopeful* instead of *presumptuous*," he shot back in a tone that would send a diabetic into a sugar shock.

Rose Marie couldn't help but laugh. "You got away with one there, buster."

Carter gave her the short version of their travel plans. "See you at the train station in three days' time."

—⁓—

Proving that Murphy's Law can rear its nasty head in any situation, Rose Marie received an unwanted phone call the next day.

"It's me, Tom," he said. "I really need to see you and talk with you."

"Well, Tom, that's just gonna have to wait two weeks—at least."

"Why?"

"Not that I have to explain myself to you," she blurted out, "but I'm going to Florida Friday morning. My train—"

"With whom?" he demanded.

"None of your business. But I will say it's with one of my good friends. *Really* good friends." *Let him stew on that*, she thought. "And before I hang up, I'll just add that the train leaves at eleven. From Trenton." Bang went the phone, ending the call.

—⁓—

Carter leaned over the edge of the train platform, all the while wondering if this trip was the right decision. Rose Marie had seemed somewhat hesitant about the impromptu vacation. He squinted through the falling snow and stared down the end of the tracks. He was waiting in Newark for the arrival of the Amtrak Silver Service from New York City. After boarding, the train would head to Orlando. On the way, it would make an all-important stop in Trenton, where Rose Marie was waiting for him.

A whistle pierced the stillness, signaling the arrival of the train. It was half an hour late thanks to the six inches of snow already on the ground. Carter maneuvered his baggage aboard and found their reserved compartment on the platform side of car number 4134. Moments later, the Florida-bound train pulled out of Newark, heading for its next stop: Trenton.

Carter watched the snow pound against the windows, matching the intensity of his heartbeat. It seemed like an eternity before the six silver cars passed Metro Park and New Brunswick. *Just under half an hour to Trenton*, he thought.

He again questioned whether he and Rose Marie were doing the right thing. Even though he was divorced and she was separated and contemplating ending her marriage, he still wasn't sure about their decision. Thank God neither of them had any children to further complicate their plans.

"This has to be right. *Right?*" he whispered. "Yes," he agreed with his reflection in the window.

Lost in his thoughts, he noticed the train was slowing. Trenton was in reach. So was Rose Marie. And despite the bad weather, the train was arriving on time.

Snow had frosted the window. His right hand swiped the glass like a windshield wiper blade. "Where is she?" he mumbled. His breath fogged the glass, momentarily ending his visual quest. His right hand cleared a one-by-two-foot swatch. Wishing he had what he called the *eyes of night*, he focused on every woman, praying each near-shapeless form was Rose Marie.

She's supposed to meet me in Trenton.

He cleared the glass again. With this second sight came a simultaneous lull in the storm. Then he saw Rose Marie huddled in a corner, seeking refuge from the blizzard. She was in a heated discussion with Tom—her husband. Carter recognized him from a photograph he had seen. Carter could hear faintly the penitent words from the Tom's lips: "I'm sorry, Rose Marie. Please give me another chance. *Please.*"

Carter banged on the window and waved at her. She glanced in his direction. His heart did another crescendo. A snowflake landed on her nose. She brushed it away and reached for her suitcases. Tom grabbed her by the elbows. He went down on one knee, pleading unheard words. Rose Marie nodded, and Tom stood. The couple kissed and then embraced. When Tom bent to pick up his wife's luggage, Rose Marie looked over his shoulder, searched for Carter behind a snow-blocked window, and mouthed two words: "I'm sorry."

Carter sighed and collapsed into his seat, tears cascading down his cheeks. He looked at the blurry bouquet of daises next to him. He selected one flower, began an age-old ritual of removing petals, and chanted "She loves me. She loves me not. She loves me. . . ."

CONTRIBUTORS

ANDRYA BAILEY is an award winning contemporary romance writer who lives in Texas, USA with her family. When she travels, she loves to visit museums and learn about art, which she usually incorporates into her stories. *Olympian Passion* is the first book in the *Olympian Love* series and it has received the 5 star seal from Readers' Favorite. The second book, *Olympian Heartache*, will be released in summer 2016. Follow her Facebook page to find out more at: https://www.facebook.com/andryabailey

---

FERN BRADY is the founder and Vice President of Inklings Publishing. She began her writing career as a foreign correspondent in Houston for the *Mexico City Daily Bulletin*. She taught for 15 years in Alief ISD and is a full-time Realtor in Houston. She was co-editor of Spider Road Press' *Eve Requiem* anthology. Her book, *Smiley Face Blattoon* written under pen name Nefari Ydarb, won 1st Place in Texas Authors Association's contest for Best Picture Book for All Ages. She enjoys a great life with her fabulous husband, Mike and their three dog-babies-Arwen, Grace and Merlin.

EDGAR COLLIE grew up in a diversely religious family during the remarkable Sixties' and mid-Seventies in San Antonio, Texas. For years, he imagined writing the Great American Novel; but perhaps guided by the spirits of his past, he's seeking to change the world with words—changing how we view sexual pleasure and erotica—the greatest things evolution ever did for us.

COPPER HAYES appreciates her senses. She filters all her experiences through a sieve that finds something exceptional to see, hear, taste, smell or feel. Especially feel. In spite of her eclectic nature, she has gathered a husband who lets her parade around in a crown (until she needs it knocked off for a spell), a houseful of beagles, a best friend who can hear anything, a colorful, comfortable home, a relatively sane extended family and a Mac Air to capture her rather offbeat personality.

ELIZABETH ANN DOMINO was born and raised in Bryan, Texas. She says she is probably the only Mexican who doesn't know how to speak Spanish. Along with her husband, she is raising a blended family of four kids while working a legitimate 9–5 job and serving as Vice President and Press Director for the Houston Writers Guild. A former staff writer for the lifestyle magazine Act Badd, her writing has also been featured in an on-campus publication, *The Bayou Review*, on the blog, *Curators of Dopeness*, as well as her own blog *Ramblings of an Ovary*. She will appear in the 2016 *Listen To Your Mother SouthEast Texas* production this April. Elizabeth started writing in college. She enrolled in a Creative Writing class in Fall of 2007, attending for the sake of fulfilling a requisite for an English credit for her Art degree. She found that writing opened her heart and she became addicted to writing. She attended workshops and joined critique groups. She started out writing dark ironic fiction and later transitioned into semi-autobiographical fiction while maintaining a personal blog on the trials and tribulations of mothering, womaning and in general living. About writing, she says, "It's tough, and I don't have the playbook with all the right moves, and I wanted to know if anyone else out there still felt like a failure. Like that 17-year-old awkward girl in Chemistry class who is always off by one misstep."

C.S. JULIA is a relentless writer who knows that a good story can bring a reader immense satisfaction and entertainment at the same time. It is her primary goal to get you excited about the joys that love, sex, and fantasy can bring to your life. She has learned that the sexiest person in the room is not necessarily the one the world considers the prettiest, but most likely the person who is the most comfortable in their own sexy skin. Be bold.

PAUL KRUMREI, JR. was born and Raised in Northern Minnesota, a transplant with a love and passion for all things art. Drawing inspiration from romantic periods in history, combining it with modern styles and art forms to create soft and tender works audiences can relate to. Paul studied Fine Arts at the College of Visual Arts in St. Paul, Minnesota shortly before it closed and further enhanced, challenged, and retaught himself everything he knew about art and design. Connection is what he strives for, whether it be creating a design, a custom piece of jewelry, a portrait painting, or perhaps even a social piece simply to convey a visual message about topics he feel strongly on. Even in different mediums, the soft tender expressions always convey the artists love... of love!

J. DENNIS PAPP, a Vietnam veteran, worked for 41 years in advertising, marketing and public relations for various multinational corporations and the Newark Public Library. His novel, *Fear Was My Only Weapon*, tells the true story of his tour in Vietnam as a personnel clerk, being forbidden to have ammo for his weapon. His other published works include numerous articles and short stories in trade magazines and newspapers, as well as inclusion in ghosts, an anthology of ethereal experiences, and several short stories (including an award-winning one), in an anthology entitled *The Collection*. A graduate of Marquette University's College of Journalism, in Milwaukee, Wisconsin, Dennis is a New Jersey native and resides in Hamilton Township with his wonderful wife, Annette, two great sons, a fantastic daughter-in-law, and a precocious granddaughter.

SUE ROMAN is a native of Wyoming and moved to Houston in 1985. She is writing her first novel *Something Bad Happened Here*, a murder mystery set in Galveston, Texas. Sue is self-employed as a media consultant and works part-time for two attorneys.

X. K. TANGLEY graduated from Rice after attending school on the East coast. Among other jobs, he's driven a carriage in Central Park (NYC), done construction on houses, been in a bumper plating factory, recycled pop bottles for plastic, surveyed subdivisions, laid out storm drains, invented types of drones, created an aircraft propulsion system with no moving parts, figured out how to analyze corrosive gases with electricity, worked as an operator in a refinery and a paper plant, run a car tune-up business, made light-emitting diodes, and sold door-to-door. Tangley is married and lives in Houston. Hobbies are reading, writing, inventing, carpentry, cars, and investing. He likes cats and travel.

DAVID WELLING is a Houston-based writer, artist, and graphic designer. His lifelong interest in movies (and the places that show them) led to the writing of *Cinema Houston: From Nickelodeon to Megaplex*, which chronicles the history of movie theatres in Texas' largest city. *Cinema Houston* is the recipient of the 2008 Julia Ideson Award from the Friends of the Texas Room, and the Society of Architectural Historians' 2009 Antoinette Forrester Downing Award. He is now writing fiction. His website and blog is davidwelling.com.

About the Houston Writers Guild

THE HOUSTON WRITERS GUILD is a community of writers of all skill levels striving to improve their craft and career through education and camaraderie.

The Guild was founded in 1998 by Roger Paulding with seven participants and has grown to more than 200 active members today. Over its first fifteen years, the Guild sponsored 36 workshops and six 2-day conferences. Roger led the group until 2013, when he passed the reins to Pamela Fagan Hutchins. On September 17, 2014, after a terrific year of leadership, Pamela passed the torch on to Fernanda Brady and Denise Satterfield. Together they are geared up to take HWG to a higher level. Their vision is, with the help of volunteers, to make the Houston Writers Guild a household name in the writing community.

The Guild offers its members workshops/conferences/webinars to learn about their craft and critique groups with excellent participant feedback. It creates opportunities to build careers through networking, as well as, opportunities for author book sales throughout the Greater Houston area and neighboring communities.

Houston Writers Guild
houstonwritersguild.org
P.O.Box 42255
Houston, TX 77242